THE MAN WHO KILLED
THE MARSHAL

His only reason for coming to this settlement at the edge of nowhere was to escape the past that his gun had blazed for him, but Dan Reneger was in trouble from the start. The Marshal knew his name— and wanted to know why he was the only man on the stage the holdup-man had left alone. And by the time he met his new partner's wife, and saw her bullied by a lawman who preferred corpses to suspects, Reneger knew that the peace he sought was still out of sight—and that he might have to kill again to find it.

THE MAN WHO KILLED THE MARSHAL

Ray Hogan

CURLEY LARGE PRINT
HAMPTON, NEW HAMPSHIRE

Library of Congress Cataloging-in-Publication Data

Hogan, Ray, 1908–
  The man who killed the marshal / Ray Hogan
    p. cm.
  ISBN 0–7927–1507–1
  ISBN 0–7927–1506–3 (pbk.)
  1. Large type books. I. Title.
[PS3558.O3473M28 1993]   92–43074
813′.54—dc20   CIP

British Library Cataloguing in Publication Data available

This Large Print edition is published by Chivers Press, England, and by Curley Large Print, an imprint of Chivers North America, 1993.

Published by arrangement with Donald MacCampbell, Inc.

U.K. Hardcover ISBN 0 7451 1839 9
U.K. Softcover   ISBN 0 7451 1849 6
U.S. Hardcover ISBN 0 7927 1507 1
U.S. Softcover   ISBN 0 7927 1506 3

Printed in Great Britain

CHAPTER ONE

Through the window of the stagecoach, Dan Reneger could see the peaks of the Escudillas reaching into the steel blue of the summer sky, as if hoping to bridge the gap between heaven and earth. *The hills of home*, he thought, as his lean body rolled with the swaying of the coach ... Only it actually wasn't home yet; rather, home it would be.

He sighed wearily, a tall, powerful man with remote, gray eyes and thick, dark hair, he was much older at twenty-six than could be expected. Hardship, disappointments, and the harsh touch of experience had all combined to lay their tempering mark upon him, but Reneger seldom thought about such things. He knew only that finally, after so long a time, he was to realize a dream—one he'd see through, regardless of the past and of the shadow that hung like a threatening cloud above him.

Always, it seemed to him, he'd wanted to have a place of his own where he could raise horses. Even now, what he'd have wouldn't be much, but it would be a beginning. It took money—quite a lot of it—to go into the business right, and a man couldn't accumulate much riding fence and hazing cattle for someone else. But he had five

1

hundred dollars tucked away in his pocketed belt, and Luke Shofner, who was to be his partner, had a similar amount.

Pooled, they'd have enough cash for grub and the gear necessary to start trapping mustangs and build a simple camp. Give them a year during which they could establish a herd by keeping the best of the stallions and mares for breeding stock, a couple more while nature took its course, and they'd have what they both had long sought—independence and a way of life each deemed most desirable.

It should work out fine. Luke was a good man at breaking wild broncs, and coupled with Dan's own knowledge of horses, the arrangement should work. That they were a bit shy on trapping experience—Reneger had spent one summer with a party of Mustangers—shouldn't prove too much of a drawback. A knowledge of the fundamentals coupled with an understanding of horses would offset that deficiency. And Luke Shofner would make a good partner. They were about the same age, thought alike, and Luke, who maybe drank a little too much on occasions, was a smiling, easygoing man not hard to be around.

They had met on Jace Organ's cattle ranch in Texas, both hiring on one spring for branding chores and winding up staying when the rancher, recognizing talent, offered them permanent berths. Each had liked the other from the start, and from then on, they'd run together, learning eventually they had mutual ambitions. The partnership was a logical result.

Leaning forward, ignoring the two men who had climbed aboard that morning at Cedar Crossing to take the seat opposite, Dan braced himself with spraddled legs as the vehicle slammed along the rutted road and continued to stare out across the gray and tan flats and foothills at the distant peaks.

He was arriving a few days early. The date for his meeting with Luke in Frisco Springs, where they planned to headquarter, had been pegged at the fifteenth, and it was only the twelfth. But he had been anxious to get on the ground, arrange for equipment and such, and be all set to pull out when Luke showed up.

Shofner had gone to pay a visit to his folks somewhere around Wichita, Kansas, and had quit Jace Organ a month early for that purpose. They were getting along in years, Luke explained, and he felt he should see them once again before tying himself down to a job that likely would keep his tail close to a saddle for a long spell.

Dan, however, had stayed on the job, electing to accumulate all cash possible. Chances were it would be late summer before they'd have any stock to sell, and he didn't want to risk running short of money and being forced into doing something contrary to their plans. They should have enough, even allowing for a few setbacks and accidents. A thousand dollars was—

'Hovendon ... Cal Hovendon.'

Dan became aware that the portly, well-dressed cattleman with the flowing moustache sitting across from him was extending his hand.

'Reneger,' he said, taking the rancher's fingers into his own.

The cattleman nodded, bucked his head at the man beside him, a small, still-faced individual wearing a well-worn pistol. 'One of my boys—Pete Oldaker.'

Oldaker moved his shoulders slightly.

'Expect you've heard of me,' Hovendon said expansively, settling back and shifting a small, black leather satchel from the seat to his lap.

Reneger said: 'Afraid not.'

The rancher's brows lifted with surprise, and a forced grin pulled at his lips. He flicked Oldaker with a glance, brought his attention back to Dan.

'Reckon that proves you're a stranger in these parts. I got the biggest spread in the country—raise some of the finest beef that ever stood on four legs.'

Dan studied Cal Hovendon quietly.

Everything the rancher owned would be the biggest and the best, he realized.

'Fact is, just coming back from selling off a thousand head of prime stuff. Got the jump on the rest of the growers, took a part of my herd in a month early.' The cattleman paused, thumped the satchel. 'Got top price that way, being the first in ... Nineteen forty a head.'

Hovendon was also a fool, shooting off his mouth about the money he was obviously carrying. But that was where Pete Oldaker came in; undoubtedly a hired gun, his job was to see that nothing happened to it.

The coach, rounding a curve in the road, tipped sharply, squealing and popping from the strain. The driver's voice sounded faintly above the racket, and dust boiled up from the spinning wheels. They dipped forward, plunged into a shallow wash, bounced up the opposite side. Hovendon peered through the window.

'Ain't much farther ... Hour or so.'

Reneger looked up hopefully. He'd been riding the board-hard cushions for days. 'That to Frisco Springs?'

Hovendon said: 'That's where I'm headed. You, too?'

Dan nodded.

'First time, eh?'

'Been through the country a couple of times.'

5

'Figure to stay?'

Irritation pricked Reneger, but the smile on the rancher's face indicated only a friendly interest and not an attempt to pry—not that it mattered particularly. And he guessed if he were to become a part of the community, he'd as well get acquainted.

'Be in and out. Aim to do some wild horse trapping farther west.'

Hovendon pursed his lips. 'Plenty of mustangs around, especially up toward the Red Butts country. Be glad to see somebody thin them out. Goddam stallions always raiding somebody's remuda, besides eating up good grass. Got a market lined up?'

'We have.'

The cattleman's eyes again flickered. 'We? Somebody going in with you? Somebody in Frisco I maybe know?'

Dan shrugged, tired of talk. Friendly interest or not, the rancher had about filled his quota of questions.

'No, stranger here, too,' he said, and leaning back, turned his eyes again to the landscape rushing past the window.

Hovendon drew a cigar from a silver case, bit off the end, struck fire to the tip. Exhaling a cloud of smoke, he said patronizingly, 'Expect I could use some good horseflesh myself. Of course, I could send some of my own boys out, round up a few, but I don't like pulling them off cattle ... You get some

6

nice stuff—really good—broke and ready to use, drive them over. I'll see if I can use them.'

Dan nodded absently.

'Ranch is east of town. Ask anybody, they can tell you where the Hovendon place is ... Got more acres of good grass than any rancher this side of the Rio Grande ... Smart I was. Rode in from Texas back in 'sixty ... Picked me a choice spot, drove off the Apaches...'

Reneger stared at the hills, now drawing nearer, becoming more distinct. Cal Hovendon liked to talk, and it was evident his favorite topic was himself. Undoubtedly, such was a well-known and accepted fact, judging from the bored look on Pete Oldaker's face.

'... Good country, all of it. Even up there where you're aiming to trap mustangs. Too rough for cattle, however. Ever do any trapping?'

Dan moved his head in the affirmative. He'd be damn glad when they reached Frisco Springs and he'd be rid of Cal Hovendon. The rancher's constant yammering was starting to wear.

'Notice you're not wearing a gun ... Be needing one where you're going. Man's close to Apache country up there in the Buttes. My advice is...'

His pistol and cartridge belt were rolled up

7

in his blanket, which, in turn, was lashed to his saddle, carried in the boot of the stagecoach. He'd quit packing a gun after that last brush with the law, concluding that to not wear a weapon was to not be tempted to use it. He guessed he'd have to strap it on once he got back in the hills.

'Obliged,' he murmured.

The coach began to slow on a grade, and thick brush loomed up on both sides of the road, hemming it in. Hovendon cleared his throat, clamped his cigar between his teeth, and brushed at the dust settling on his broadcloth coat. He glanced out the window.

'Anson's Pass,' he said. 'Once we're on top, it'll be downhill all the way.'

The cattleman was like a guide, pointing out every landmark ... Salvation Peak ... Pinon Knob ... Tyson's Wash ... the Tularosa Hills ... Lost Lake ... Maybe he should be grateful, Dan thought. Next time he made the trip, he'd know the country by name.

Abruptly, the coach began to slow. Brakes screeched as they jammed against iron wheels. The vehicle faltered, came to a stop. Hovendon frowned angrily, turned to look through the window. He drew back hastily as the muzzle of a pistol was thrust into his face.

'Everybody—pile out!' a muffled voice ordered.

CHAPTER TWO

'Holdup!' Hovendon breathed in a disbelieving voice. 'By God—a holdup!' He threw a stern glance to Oldaker. 'Start earning your money, Mister.'

The gunman's lips tightened, and his bleak features became grim. Reaching for the handle, he opened the door, stepped slowly into the sunlight, still filled with spinning particles of dust. The rancher bobbed his head at Dan.

'Go on.'

Reneger shrugged, followed Oldaker, his nerves taut as the possibility of losing the money belt and its hard-earned contents stabbed at his consciousness, set up a strong worry ... If he lost that—

Arms lifted, he halted beside the gunman and narrowly eyed the outlaw, a tall, thin man wearing a white cloth wrapped about his head. A battered hat was pulled low, and a yellow slicker hung to his ankles. At that moment, Dan heard Hovendon move in behind him. The rancher had left his satchel inside the coach, he noted, and wished there had been some way he might have ditched his money also.

The outlaw backed away slowly. 'Climb down,' he said then to the driver, his words almost unintelligible because of the mask.

The driver swung from his perch, taking considerable time. Hands stretched high above his head, he crossed to where Dan and the others stood, walking with the hesitant lameness of age. Sanford, Hovendon had called him. Otey Sanford.

'Don't know why'n hell you're stopping me,' he complained in a cracked voice. 'Ain't carrying no strong box.'

'You got something better, Pop,' the highwayman said. 'A fat rancher.'

Cal Hovendon moaned softly. The outlaw pointed with his free hand to the opposite side of the road.

'Any of you feel like getting real brave,' he said, 'there's a friend of mine standing there in the brush with a scatter gun. Just figured I ought to tell you.'

Dan glanced to the undergrowth beyond the coach. Well back and almost completely hidden, he could see a blur of faded cloth—a jacket, apparently. Above it, he made out the shape of a hat. The foliage was so thick he could determine nothing else.

Bringing his attention back to the masked outlaw, he studied the man warily. When he came in close, tried to take the money belt, he'd jump him—shotgun or not. By moving fast, he could throw the outlaw against the coach, get the vehicle between himself and the man in the brush, have time, perhaps, to get his hands on a gun. He wasn't giving up a dream so easily—not yet.

The bandit turned to Hovendon, his slicker making a dry, crackling sound as he walked. Halting in front of the rancher, he thrust out his hand.

'I'll take that money you're carrying.'

Sweat was standing in large beads on the rancher's forehead. His mouth worked convulsively. 'Money? I ain't got no money—only a few dollars. You're welcome to—'

The outlaw wagged his head. 'Sure hate to see a grown man squirm. I'm meaning the twenty thousand you got for your cows.'

'Twenty thousand! Hell, man, I—'

'Thereabouts, so I heard.'

Hovendon's agitated face glistened in the driving sunlight. 'I ain't got it! Left it in the bank—'

'Don't give me that!' the outlaw snarled, abruptly out of patience. 'Fork over, Mister, I ain't wasting no more time!'

'Go ahead—search me. Look for yourself.'

The masked man shrugged. 'Don't figure there's a need. Was I you, I'd've left it in the coach—hid out ... Get it.'

The rancher looked around desperately. His flared eyes touched Oldaker and then narrowed. Shoulders going down, he nodded.

'All right, but I'm warning you—you ain't

11

getting away with this. I swing a lot of weight in this country. I'll have every lawman—'

'Expect you sure will,' the outlaw drawled. 'Get it! Rest of you,' he added suddenly as Sanford shifted wearily, 'just keep reaching.'

Reneger remained motionless, eyes following every move of the highwayman. So far, the masked man had paid no attention to him, seemed interested only in Cal Hovendon. Silent, he waited, watched.

The bandit raised his pistol slightly. 'I'll say it once more, then—'

A dry sob wrenched from the rancher's throat. He seemed to wilt, grow small as he turned to Oldaker.

'On the floor—under the seat.'

The gunman glanced to the outlaw for approval. The masked man nodded slightly. 'Keep remembering that shotgun. Take it slow and easy.'

Pete Oldaker, arms still up, pivoted to the coach. Reaching in with great deliberateness, he procured the satchel, started to wheel. His right arm swept down suddenly. The outlaw's weapon blasted through the hot silence, sent up a chain of rolling echoes.

Oldaker buckled, gun and satchel dropping from nerveless fingers. He staggered toward the rear wheel of the vehicle, caught at it, missed, and fell. Hovendon swore wildly.

Cool, the outlaw waggled his pistol at

12

Reneger. 'Kick it over here . . . Careful, now.'

Dan dropped back a step, caught the satchel with his toe, booted it to where the masked man stood. He slid a glance to the second outlaw in the brush. The odds were worse now. He'd be caught between the two, but with a little luck—

The bandit bent his knees, never lowering his weapon, reached down, and claimed the satchel. Not opening it, he felt its contents through the soft leather, satisfied himself that it contained the money.

'All of you—turn around,' he ordered.

'What for?' Hovendon demanded in a harried voice. 'You got the money. What else you aim to do?'

'Just making sure.'

'That mean you're going to shoot—cut us down in cold blood? No sense—'

Reneger and Otey Sanford wheeled. The rancher followed, protesting steadily. Dan felt the outlaw's hands press against him as they sought a weapon, then move on to Otey. There was a thud as the driver's pistol was tossed into the brush. The sound was echoed a moment later when Cal Hovendon's weapon fell near it.

'Start walking . . . Back down the road.'

Relief flowed through Dan Reneger. The outlaw, apparently believing him to be no more than an itinerant cowhand, was passing him by, satisfied to take only Hovendon's

13

money. Immediately, he moved off along the deep-cut ruts, anxious to get away before the highwayman had second thoughts. Sanford fell in behind him, grumbling and cursing with each step.

The rancher hung back uncertainly for a long moment, and then he, too, wheeled about, headed onto the road. Dan glanced over his shoulder. The outlaw, not relaxing his vigilance, was bending down. He picked up Oldaker's fallen weapon, hurled it after the others.

'What the hell's he figuring to do?' Hovendon wondered anxiously. 'You think he'll open up, start shooting?'

Two quick gunshots and a shout, followed by the rattle of chains and pound of hooves, answered the rancher's question. They halted, turned. The coach team, frightened by the outlaw, lunged forward in the harness, broke into a hard gallop.

'Runaway!' Otey Sanford groaned, watching the swaying coach thunder off. 'Danged jugheads won't stop 'til they reach town—if they ever do.'

The bandit was trotting toward his partner waiting in the brush. Reaching the fringe, he halted, looked back. Raising his pistol, he pressed off a shot. The bullet dug sand at the feet of the three men—a clear warning to keep their distance.

A moment later, he had ducked into the

dense undergrowth and disappeared.

CHAPTER THREE

Reneger hurried to Oldaker, knelt beside him. The gunman was dead, the bullet probably bringing instant death.

'First time, by God!' he heard Otey Sanford mutter. 'First time they ever held me up.'

Thankful, Dan rose to his feet, stared off into the brush. He'd been lucky. The outlaws had passed him by. Tension began to drain from his body.

'Come on!' Cal Hovendon yelled from the edge of the road. 'Got to stop—'

The faint rap of a running horse broke into his urgent words, silenced them. The sound died quickly, and the cattleman began to swear in a low, harsh monotone. Dan stared at the rancher; Pete Oldaker's death meant nothing to him—only the money counted. He turned, looked off down the road. Whorls of dust hung motionless in the heat in the wake of the runaway team.

Sanford said: 'Might as well start walking.'

Reneger nodded, swung his gaze back to the brush. He frowned. The patch of cloth—the second outlaw—was still there. Suspicious, he cut away from the road,

15

bulled his way through the undergrowth to where the cloth was, jerked it free. There had been no man hiding in the thick brush—only a faded, worn shirt arranged with a discarded hat to resemble one. Carrying the articles back to the road, he dropped them at Hovendon's feet.

'He was alone.'

The rancher began to swear again. 'And we let him get away with it!'

'Not much we could do.'

'Could've tried—rushed him, maybe. If all of us had—'

'There'd been somebody besides Pete laying there dead,' Otey said dryly.

'Leastways, he tried.'

'Oldaker was a fool, drawing on a man holding a cocked pistol,' Dan said.

'The God's truth,' Otey agreed. 'What'll we do about him?'

Reneger pointed to a low embankment a few yards away. 'Put him there, pull brush over him. Soon as we get to town, we can send somebody back.'

Sanford nodded. Bending over, he thrust his hands into the gunman's armpits. Dan took the dead man's legs, and together they carried him to the ledge and covered him with leafy branches.

'No varmints going to bother him long as it's light,' the old driver said, mopping at his face.

16

Hovendon, waiting impatiently, hawked, spat. 'Come on, let's get started. Want to get Trask on that bastard's trail soon as I can.'

'Reckon we're ready,' Sanford answered, and stepping in beside Reneger, moved off into the road.

The sun was beating down with full intensity, and by the time they reached the summit of the pass, little more than a half mile distant, all were sweat-soaked and heaving for breath. Halting, Dan and Sanford settled down upon a fallen pine to rest. Hovendon, moving about restlessly, remained in the center of the road.

'Ought to be somebody showing up,' he said peevishly. 'Ain't far from town.'

Otey scratched at his chin. 'Hardly been time enough ... And if that coach turned over, piled up in the ditch, there ain't no use looking.'

The rancher stared into the distance. 'Be just my luck,' he muttered. 'Let's go.'

Sanford got to his feet. Reneger followed but paused as he became aware of Hovendon's frowning study. He gave the rancher a questioning glance.

'Something on your mind?'

Cal Hovendon shifted his shoulders, turned away, and moved off into the road. They were over the hump now, and it was downgrade, easier going. There was larger timber in evidence, also—pines, spruce, a

17

smattering of fir—and the air seemed cooler.

'Listen!' Otey said abruptly, coming to a halt. 'Could be them coming now.'

Dan paused. The hollow thud of oncoming horses was a faint drumming in the stillness. Grateful that the long, hot walk was ending almost before it got started, he crossed to the edge of the road, settled himself upon a flat rock to wait. Sanford joined him, but the rancher elected to remain where he had stopped. Minutes later, the coach swept into view. Otey squinted through the haze.

'It's Amos—Amos Venn,' he said. 'Reckon the station agent sent him after us. That there's the marshal setting next him. Name of Trask.'

The stage rolled to a rocking halt. The driver, a white-haired oldster with a stained beard and trailing moustache, cocked his head to one side, grinned broadly at Sanford.

'Comes a time when a man's so old he lets his team get away from him, I figure he ought—'

'Go to hell,' Otey said amiably, drawing back from the cloud of dust swirling from under the wheels. 'We was held up—robbed.'

Venn sobered. Trask climbed down from the box. He was a big man with a ruddy complexion matched by thinning red hair, giving him a sort of peeled look. His small, black, agate eyes darted back and forth, and his mouth was scarcely more than a straight, colorless line ... A tough one, Dan concluded.

'Held up?' he echoed, looking directly at Cal Hovendon.

'You're goddam right!' the rancher replied in an accusing tone. 'Hell of a note when a man can't travel in his own backyard without having a gun stuck in his face.'

'Been no holdups around here for years,' the Marshal said coldly.

'Ain't all,' Sanford said. 'Pete Oldaker's laying back there a piece—dead.'

Trask's expression hardened. 'How'd that happen?'

'Went for his iron, outlaw cut him down,' Hovendon said, fine drawn by impatience. 'Let's get to town. Want a posse put together so's we can start looking for that sonofabitch.'

Ignoring the rancher, Trask turned slowly to Reneger. 'Who're you?'

The towering arrogance of the lawman rubbed at Dan's nerves. 'Name's Reneger,' he said stiffly.

'You a passenger?'

The answer was obvious, but Dan nodded.

'Going where?'

'Frisco Springs.'

'Ain't no sense standing here in this heat,'

19

Otey broke in, and then glancing hastily at Trask, added in a different tone: 'Why don't we load in, do our talking in the shade? Got to go get Oldaker's body, anyway.'

The lawman's hard eyes were bright. 'You and Amos get in. I ain't through yet.'

Reneger shook his head. 'Had all the standing on my feet I want,' he drawled, turning to the coach. 'You got questions to ask me, let's do it setting down.'

'I said we'd wait!'

Dan opened the door, pulled himself into the shadowed interior, settled himself on the seat. He looked back, lips parted in a deceptive smile. Trask was staring at him, anger coloring his features. Hovendon and Otey watched in silence.

'Come on,' Reneger invited lazily. 'That sun's pure hell.'

Immediately, Cal Hovendon moved to the step. Otey, face tipped down, began to climb the wheel to the driver's perch. Trask remained motionless for several long moments and then followed the rancher into the vehicle. Jaw set, he leaned forward, eyes drilling into Reneger.

'Friend, next time I tell you to do something—'

The coach lunged forward and tipped as it cut back into the road. Trask caught himself, temper again gripping him tight. Bracing himself, he continued to stare at Dan until

20

the stage was under way, and then pushed back, turned to Hovendon.

'Got any idea who the holdup man was?'

The cattleman shook his head. 'Wore a yellow slicker. Had a rag of some kind pulled over his face. Only his eyes were showing.'

'Voice sound like somebody you know?'

'Couldn't tell nothing about it. Muffled.'

'Well, what about his horse?' the lawman demanded irritably. 'There a brand on it?'

'Never saw it. Had it stashed in the brush. Heard him ride off, that's all.'

'Only one man?'

Hovendon nodded. 'We figured there was two of them. Fooled us with an old shirt and hat hung in the brush.'

Trask considered that in silence as the coach rolled on. After a time, he raised his eyes to Reneger.

'You see anything special?'

'No more than he did. Couldn't tell much about the man. Was tall.'

'How much did you lose?'

'Never bothered me. Seems he was only after Hovendon's cash.'

The rancher leaned forward. 'Something I been wondering about. Was only me that got robbed. Paid no mind to Reneger—'

'Or the driver,' Dan added.

Trask's gaze was a steady, pushing force. 'You carrying any money?'

'Some.'

'How much is some?'

'Few hundred dollars.'

'And that owlhoot never made you fork over?'

'Didn't even ask him to,' Hovendon pointed out.

'Don't that seem sort of funny to you, Marshal?'

For a time, there was only the steady drum of the horses, the whine of the wheels, and then Trask, resting his elbows on his knees, said: 'You explain why, Mister?'

Reneger crossed his arms, shook his head in disgust. 'Maybe I don't look prosperous.'

The cattleman grunted in dissatisfaction. 'Sure seems mighty funny to me.'

The coach began to slow. Dan glanced out the window. They were back to where the holdup had occurred. Venn shouted something, and the team wheeled about in a tight circle and came to a stop. Trask climbed over Hovendon, dropped down onto the road, stood aside while Venn and Otey Sanford loaded the gunman's body into the boot. Then, followed by Sanford, he returned to his seat. The old driver settled next to Dan while, on top, Amos Venn shouted at the horses, set the coach to moving again.

At once, Trask said: 'Reneger, been thinking about what Cal told me. You sure there wasn't something familiar to that road

22

agent?'

'Damn sure,' Dan snapped. 'What're you getting at? You trying to say I had something to do with it?'

'Wondering just that,' the Marshal replied coolly. 'Could've been you are partners.'

Reneger stared at the lawman, then laughed. 'Sure. I stood right there with my hands up, watched him take the money and ride off. And now I'm still waiting around.'

'He ain't even wearing a gun!' Otey put in, frowning.

Trask favored the driver with a hard glance. 'Could have been set up—you riding along, making sure everything went right,' he said, coming back to Dan. 'You could meet up later.'

There was still humor in the suggestion to Dan Reneger. He shrugged. 'You're good at cooking up cock and bull yarns, Marshal, but you're way off. Was I in a holdup where twenty thousand dollars was grabbed, I'd stay mighty close to it 'til I got my share.'

The lawman's brows lifted. 'How'd you know there was twenty thousand dollars?'

'Hovendon mentioned it ... Fact is, I got his life's story ... All of it.'

Trask grunted in disgust, shook his head wearily at the cattleman. 'Just the same,' he said slowly, 'I ain't so sure. Where'd you say you was headed?'

'Same place as before—Frisco Springs.'

23

Temper was rising slowly within Reneger. He'd held himself back from the moment the lawman had begun to question him, but matters were beginning to wear thin. He had taken an immediate dislike to Trask; everything about the Marshal irritated him—the man's appearance, his attitude, and now his ridiculous suspicions. But he'd keep a tight rein on himself; he couldn't afford to get crosswise with the law.

'Staying over?'

'Aims to trap mustangs. Up in the Red Butte country,' Hovendon volunteered. 'Anyway, that's what he claims.'

'Just what I'll be doing,' Dan said quietly. 'Expect to be in and out of town regular.'

He paused, turned his eyes to the window, fighting to suppress the anger that refused to cool. 'And I expect to get along with everybody—you included, Marshal. One thing, however. Never was much of a hand to get pushed around.'

Trask's eyes narrowed. 'Meaning?'

'Climb off my back. You're barking at the wrong fox. Best thing you can do is get yourself a tracker, hightail it to where the holdup took place—and start trailing. You're wasting time asking me questions.'

24

CHAPTER FOUR

Trask's lips tightened, and his eyes filled with a strange, hard glitter. Hovendon remained absolutely quiet, his body rocking with the motion of the coach. It was Otey Sanford who broke the charged silence. He glanced out the window, spoke hurriedly.

'Reckon we're here.'

The lawman eased back as the stage whirled around a corner, came to a sliding halt in front of the Mogollon Hotel. Reneger, with great deliberation, every part of his body a study in careful, precise movement, opened the door, stepped out, fully aware of the lawman's hard stare. He still simmered with anger, but he was holding firm, not giving in to the hot urgency clamoring within himself. He'd pass it all—say no more, do nothing. Let it go ... He'd be a damned fool to start trouble.

Circling the vehicle, he stopped at the rear, found Otey and Amos Venn there ahead of him. The old driver gave him a searching look, smiled.

'Saddle and blanket all you got. Right?'

Reneger nodded, helped the man pull the heavy hull and canvas roll from the compartment. Venn and two bystanders were removing Pete Oldaker's body. Dan

25

gazed at the bleak, weathered facade of the Mogollon.

'This the best place to bed down?'

'Only place,' the driver said. 'Unless you want a back room in the Nugget,' he added, pointing to a large saloon on the opposite side of the street.

'No thanks,' Dan said, and slinging his gear over his shoulder, started for the hotel's porch.

Trask and Cal Hovendon were there before him, the center of a rapidly gathering crowd. Two men in business suits were hurrying up, and a third, carrying a small, black bag, was slanting for the rear of the stagecoach. Amos Venn's voice slowed his pace to a walk.

'Won't be needing you, Doc. Pete's dead.'

Reneger stepped up onto the veranda, halted as Trask separated from the gathering, moved in to intercept him. Dan sighed, dropped the saddle to the rough boards, wheeled to face the lawman.

A hush fell over the crowd. Trask crossed his arms, thrust his head forward. 'Ain't done with you yet, Reneger. Don't go getting ideas about leaving town.'

'Wasn't what I had in mind,' Dan replied in slow spaced words. 'But I don't reckon it makes any difference. You're through with me, all right. Time comes when I'm ready to go—I'll go.'

'The hell you will! If I tell you—'

'You want to jail me, let's hear a charge,' Dan cut in. 'I don't mean some trumped up pipe dream like you had there on the stagecoach. I mean something that makes sense.'

Trask flicked the silent crowd with a nervous glance. One of the men in a business suit pushed forward a step, frowning.

'What's this, Marshal?'

Trask's shoulders relaxed. 'Not sure he wasn't in on the holdup, that's all.'

'I wasn't,' Reneger snapped. 'Any fool can see that.'

The older man turned to Trask. 'If you've got proof of some kind that makes you think he was, arrest him. You know the law.'

The Marshal's eyes never shifted from Reneger. 'Just a hunch,' he murmured.

Dan grinned sardonically, reached for his gear, and hoisted it to his shoulder. Without so much as a glance at the lawman and the hushed crowd, he pivoted and entered the hotel. As he passed through the doorway into the shadowy lobby, filled with the day's trapped heat, he heard Trask say something. His step slowed, and then he continued on to the desk, where a balding clerk awaited him, refusing to trust himself further.

The room overlooked the street. Tossing his gear into a corner, Dan stripped, washed himself, shaved, and began to pull on clean

27

clothing. Hesitating, he crossed to the window, drew aside the curtain, and studied curiously the dusty strip below.

The Nugget Saloon ... Lavendar's General Store ... Venn's Livery Stable ... A dozen other establishments—it looked like a pretty good town ... His drifting gaze halted on a cluster of horsemen gathering in front of the Marshal's office. Trask was assembling his posse.

'Luck,' he said, half aloud, and came back to the center of the room and finished dressing.

Running down the bandit would be quite a chore. Covered and masked as he had been, there was nothing in the way of identification to go on. Finding him through his horse was also out. Chances were good Cal Hovendon had seen the last of his twenty thousand dollars. As for himself—luck had smiled on him for a change.

Going down the stairs, he crossed the lobby and paused. He was anxious to start things moving, get all in readiness for departure when Luke Shofner arrived ... First thing would be a horse for himself; then the pack mules. Locating the livery stable, he stepped off the porch, waded through the ankle-deep dust for that building. Farther down, Trask and Hovendon, leading the party of riders, were just pulling out.

Reaching the livery barn, he turned into

the office. Amos Venn looked up from a battered desk, said: 'Be with you in a min—' and stopped short. He rose hurriedly, came forward. 'Something I can do for you?'

Reading the frown on Dan's face, he grinned, added: 'Was just helping out the station agent, driving the stagecoach. This is my place. You wanting a horse?'

'If you've got a good one.'

'Renting or buying?'

'Buying. Something with plenty of bottom. Be using him hard.'

Venn rubbed at his jaw. 'Got a bay gelding. Expect he'd be the best.'

Reneger nodded and followed Venn to a corral at the rear of the barn, where a dozen or so horses dozed in the afternoon sun. The stableman pointed to a tall, dark one with a white blaze.

'How's that'n look to you?'

Dan opened the gate, entered the yard. Crossing to the bay, he gave the animal a careful going over. After a time, he turned to Venn. 'Wind broke?'

The older man's face clouded indignantly. 'Him wind broke! Mister, you trying to make me mad? You think I'd palm off—'

'You'll get him back damn quick if he is. How much?'

Venn again clawed at his jaw. 'Expect I'll have to ask a hundred. Good stock and—'

'Seventy-five, and it's a deal.'

29

'Sold,' the stableman said promptly. 'Anything else?'

'Pack mules. Be needing four, along with riggings.'

Venn bobbed his head. 'I'll treat you right there, too. Aim to do your trapping alone?'

'Partner's coming in the next few days. He can pick his own horse if he don't already have one.'

Venn said, 'Fine. Be glad to deal with him, too, if he's in the market.' Stepping back, he allowed Dan to come through the gate and start for the barn. 'You get things patched up with the Marshal?'

'Nothing to patch up,' Reneger said flatly.

'Sounded like he was telling you not to leave town.'

'I'll pull out when I'm ready.'

Venn halted, laid a hand on Reneger's arm. 'Maybe it ain't none of my business, but I think you ought to know about Emil Trask.'

'Know him about as well as I want to.'

'Could be. Just wanted to say Emil's a right hard case. He gets it in for a man, he can sure be mean—and it kind of looks like he's setting things up that way for you. Reckon there ain't no man ever talked to him the way you did—nobody still alive, anyway.'

'Sounds like he might run this town to suit himself.'

'Pretty much. Sam Lavendar—he was the

30

one talking to him when you was on the porch—he's about the only one who can do anything with him. Sam owns the general store. Emil's been marshal here for quite a spell.'

'Still don't make him a king,' Reneger said and dismissed the subject. 'Want pay for that horse now?'

'Your word's good, and I'd as soon wait 'til I get them mules lined up. Can make one bill of it that way. I ain't so good at bookkeeping.'

Returning to the street, Dan dug into his pocket for the list of items and food articles he'd been compiling during spare moments for the past month. He'd as well get that handled, too. Crossing the street, he entered Lavendar's. The storekeeper greeted him impersonally.

'Be obliged if you'll get this stuff together,' Reneger said, passing the list to him. 'Pick it up in a couple of days.'

Lavendar glanced over the items. 'Have it ready by closing time, if you say.'

Dan gave the merchant a keen look, not missing the hidden meaning in his words. He smiled. 'No rush. Don't figure on pulling out until the end of the week.'

'Still be ready tonight,' Lavendar said, turning back into the aisle behind his counter. 'Just in case you change your mind.'

A man caught in the middle, Dan thought,

31

and retraced his steps to the street ... That much was done, and there was little more left to do until Luke showed up. Together, they could then complete the final details.

He glanced to the sun. Getting late. He realized suddenly that he was hungry and not a little tired. Swinging off the landing, he pointed for the Nugget ... A couple of drinks, a meal at the Frisco Springs Café, and then bed would feel good. Tomorrow, he'd haul his gear over to Venn's, try out the bay.

The Nugget had few customers. Halting at the bar, Dan ordered a whiskey, hooked his elbows on the counter's edge, and looked out over the high-ceilinged room. A half dozen men scattered about smiled, nodded pleasantly. A portly individual with a gold watch chain looped across his paunch strolled up, extended his hand.

'Name's Jess Pogue. Own the Nugget. Always like to welcome strangers personally.'

Reneger could feel the man's eyes raking him closely, searching, making their assessment. 'Glad to meet you,' he said. 'Quiet in here.'

'Posse,' Pogue explained. 'Marshal drafted everybody handy. Understand you were on that stage with Hovendon and Pete Oldaker.'

Dan signalled the bartender for a refill. 'Your marshal even figures I had something to do with the holdup.'

'So I heard,' Pogue murmured, and hurriedly backed away from the subject. 'Staying long?'

'Be in and out, if things go right,' Reneger said. He had not missed the saloonkeeper's show of caution and wondered where the man stood with Emil Trask. The lawman evidently exercised a powerful influence over the settlement—one that amounted to fear, almost. Draining his glass, he set it on the counter, reached into his pocket for a coin.

'On the house,' Pogue said, smiling. 'Custom of mine.'

'Obliged,' Dan said, and nodding to the man, walked back to the street.

The meal at the café was no better than ordinary, but it tasted good to Dan Reneger. He dawdled over it, enjoying a second piece of pie and several extra cups of coffee while he watched the bright sunlight gradually fade, turn to gold on the shop windows, and finally die entirely.

A faint breeze came down the street, whipping small whirlwinds into spinning life. Somewhere, a church bell began to toll, and a woman hurried by, half dragging a small child by the hand as she rushed homeward to prepare the evening meal.

Two punchers entered from the south, rode direct to the Nugget, dismounted, and shambled through the swinging doors on saddle-bowed legs. People were beginning to make their appearance along the walks, where lamps now laid their mellow glow against the coming night.

Dan rose, paid his check, and sauntered into the open, wondering idly how Emil Trask and the posse were faring. He hoped well; if the lawman could capture the outlaw, he'd be satisfied, forget about him. But the thought held slim promise. The holdup man had followed a carefully worked out plan.

Moving on, he walked the length of Frisco Springs's one street, doubled back, and halted in front of the hotel. He spent another ten minutes lounging in one of the veranda chairs, and then thoroughly sleepy, arose and entered the dimly lit lobby. At once, a tall figure came from the depths of the room, advancing slowly. Dan pulled up short in surprise.

Luke Shofner...

CHAPTER FIVE

At a sign from Cal Hovendon, Trask lifted his hand and brought the posse to a halt.

'Here's the place,' the rancher said as the swirling dust began to subside. He pointed to a lump of rags lying on the shoulder of the road. 'There's the old shirt and hat he used to make us think he had a partner standing in the brush.'

The lawman dismounted, strode to the garments, retrieved them. Examining both briefly, he wadded them into a knot, crammed it into a pocket of his saddlebags.

'Where was his horse?'

Havendon waved indefinitely at the undergrowth to their left. 'In there, somewheres.'

Trask swung onto his mount, touched the men on the road with a scowling glance. 'String out, start working the brush. Want to find the place where that horse was standing,' he said, and moved off.

There was a moment of confused milling as the riders sorted themselves, and then, in skirmish line formation, they followed the lawman. Almost at once, a yell went up from a man near the end.

'Over here, Marshal!'

Trask wheeled sharp right, spurred his horse to get in front of the posse, now swinging hurriedly toward the summons.

'Keep back, goddammit!' he shouted. 'Don't want them tracks all trampled to hell.'

He looked ahead, saw Tom Brookfield standing at the edge of an oak thicket. The ground within the small pocket was well marked, which would indicate that the outlaw's horse had remained there for some time. Halting, Trask came off his saddle and avoiding hoof prints and droppings alike, moved forward carefully.

'Looks like he was tied up here most of the morning,' Brookfield observed.

Trask did not bother to reply. Circling the thicket slowly, eyes on the spongy soil, he checked abruptly on the far side. Tracks led out from that point, plainly going north. The lawman grunted, stared off into that direction.

'What I told you,' Hovendon said, breaking into his thought. 'Went north.'

Unreasonable impatience ripped through Emil Trask. Stupid goddam remark! Of course the outlaw headed north—he knew that. But it was necessary to find just where, start from that exact point. For a smart man who'd made a pile of money, Cal Hovendon was as dumb as they came. Fact that he was forever shooting off his mouth, letting the whole country know all about his affairs, proved it. Always trying to impress somebody, set himself up as being so high and mighty.

Abruptly, he spun, returned to his horse, and climbed aboard. 'Keep strung out,' he ordered tersely. 'And watch for a rider. I'll take care of the tracks.'

The outlaw would be difficult to follow. The ground was hard in places, covered most of the time with dead leaves and other litter. But he had a beginning—and the general direction.

He rode on, maintaining a short distance in front of the others, eyes on the trail. Now and then, he picked up a single print. Occasionally, there was a broken branch, a trampled clump of brush ... So far so good ...

Trask slid a glance to the men flung out to either side. They were watching him, aware that he was on the killer's tracks, that for the present they need only keep pace. That was the way he liked it—being up ahead, leading a manhunt.

Emil was an old hand at it. For 20 years, he'd worn a badge, most of that time being right there in Frisco Springs. He liked the work, enjoyed being in the business of keeping law and order, and he knew he never wanted to be anything other than a lawman.

Authority was a part of his nature, his makeup, as natural as the hair that grew on his body, and he took the duties and responsibilities of his job as a way of life. Always he'd been a hunter of sorts; for game as a boy, for men when he grew up. It was something he understood, and he knew he was good at it.

That he had engendered a considerable amount of dislike and downright hate during the passage of time disturbed him not at all. Actually, he expected it, considered it a sort of tribute and a part of the price he paid for being a good lawman. He had authority, and he used it, despite men like Sam Lavendar, who were always urging caution, hinting every so often that he use gentler methods. What the hell was eating them, anyway? If he didn't use an iron hand, he wouldn't last long. They ought to realize that.

He lost the outlaw's trail a half hour later on a long, rocky slope that fed down from the mountain to their right. Pulling up, he studied the land ahead. On the yonder side of the slope were more trees. To the left and a distance from the grove's end lay the town—a place the outlaw would certainly avoid. At such times a stranger was always suspect.

Chances were he'd not cut west into Arizona and Apache country. He'd be a fool to risk it. East? Possible, but the going would be slow and hard because of the high mountains and the lack of trails. And on the other side there wasn't much—Socorro, a good 150 miles away, would be the first settlement he'd encounter, and Trask doubted if the man was equipped for such an arduous trip.

He'd continue north. There were settlements scattered along the route where supplies would be available. He would be pointing for Santa Fe, or maybe Denver ... Or he could be trying for a point even farther—Wyoming or Montana or the

Dakotas. The surprising thing was that he had not lined out for the Mexican border. Most of them did.

Goading his horse, Trask moved out onto the slope, crossed at a brisk trot, and halted when he reached the fringe of trees. Then, eyes again on the softer ground, he began a slow tour of the edge. There would be hoof prints leading into the area. The outlaw was taking no pains to conceal his movements. Either he was a fool or—

'There's a horse!'

Trask's head came up at the shout. He threw a glance at the posse member who had sung out, followed the man's pointing finger ... A buckskin grazing in a coulee. The lawman drew his pistol.

'Fan out!' he ordered. 'Circle him.'

There could have been an accident. Perhaps the outlaw had been thrown and now lay in the bushes, waiting, prepared to make a last-ditch stand. Trask licked his dry lips expectantly. There was no doubt the buckskin was the horse the fugitive had been riding; hoof prints led straight into the hollow.

The net formed, closed in. There was no one in the brush, only the horse. Disappointed, Trask climbed down, moved up to the buckskin. At that moment, Harry Wills pushed forward.

'Seen that horse before. This morning.'

Trask spun to the rider. 'Where?'

'Standing back of Grissom's place.'

Grissom ran a small saloon at the north end of town. 'You sure of that?'

'Sure as I know my own name. Recollect that saddle. All tore up so bad there ain't hardly nothing left but the horn.'

Hovendon grinned broadly. 'Reckon that ties it down, Emil. Man who owns that horse is the one who robbed me.'

But Trask, again ignoring the rancher, was already on his mount and pulling away.

'Bring that horse,' he directed as he broke out of the coulee and cut toward Frisco Springs.

It was full dark when they reached Grissom's. Followed by the entire posse, the lawman entered the dimly lit saloon. Halting in the center of the room, he glanced over the sparse crowd. Most of the customers were at the bar. A card game was in progress in a back corner. Grissom only just got by; the bulk of the trade went to Jess Pogue at the Nugget.

'Who's the owner of a buckskin wearing a Box K brand?'

At the sound of Trask's roughly put question, all eyes turned to him. A young puncher sitting in on the card game pushed back his chair.

'Me. Why?'

The Marshal's pistol came into his hand

smoothly as he squared himself about.

'I'm arresting you for the holdup of the northbound stagecoach this morning. And for killing Pete Oldaker.'

The puncher's jaw sagged. He stared at Trask and then at the men around the table. 'You loco or something, Marshal? I been right here all day.'

Grissom, a thin, sickly man with a hacking cough, came from behind his bar. 'It's the way he says. Ain't hardly left that chair. Must be some mistake.'

The man sitting next the young rider bobbed his head. 'Got to be. I know. I been playing poker with him since about daylight.'

Anger and embarrassment rushed through Emil Trask. The outlaw had apparently only borrowed the buckskin as a means for confusing his trail, while he saved his own horse for the final flight. He'd played the lawman for a sucker, forced him into a position where he looked a fool. Still ... There could be more to it ...

'Get up!' he snapped, motioning to the puncher with his pistol.

The rider rose slowly. 'What for? I ain't had nothing to do with no holdup. You heard what everybody said.'

Trask's voice was low. 'Maybe you loaned your horse. You got some way to prove you didn't? Was your buckskin the outlaw used.'

'What?'

'Won't say it again. I'm locking you up until I can get to the bottom—'

Grissom took a step forward. 'Now, Marshal, you can't—'

'The hell I can't!' Trask snarled, knocking the saloonman aside with a sweep of his arm. Anger rocking him, he took a long stride, caught the puncher by the collar, and jerked him away from the table.

The young rider, struggling to regain his balance, grabbed for the back of his chair. Trask's hand came up swiftly, struck the man a savage blow across the side of the head with his pistol.

'Goddam you—don't try fighting me!'

The puncher's knees buckled. The lawman hit him a second time, brought a flow of blood to his cheek.

Two of the men at the table came upright. Trask checked them with a warning glance. 'Stay out of this!' he shouted. 'Or, by God, I'll—'

Abruptly, his words ended. He straightened, his breath coming in deep gasps. Supporting the young puncher by the strength of his left hand, he looked around the room, eyes defiant, jaw set, challenge issuing from him.

'Locking him up, like I said,' he announced, his tone almost conversational, now that the wild anger had dissipated. 'Few things need going into.'

One of the cardplayers shook his head slowly, wonderingly. 'Pretty rough handling, Marshal—and he was telling you the truth. Can't see where you got a right to hold him.'

'My business,' Trask snapped. 'And I'll be looking up some of the rest of you, too. Be damned sure you don't leave town without seeing me first.'

'But I got a job—'

'Ain't nothing to me,' the lawman said, starting for the door with his prisoner. 'You be here when I want you.'

CHAPTER SIX

Dan Reneger's lips split with pleasure. Thrusting out his hand, he strode forward to meet Shofner.

'Didn't expect to see you yet!'

'Got my visiting done quick,' Luke replied. 'How's it go?'

'Fine. Most everything's ready. Got the mules lined up along with grub and gear.'

Shofner nodded. 'Means we can pull out about any time.'

'All we've got to do is load,' Dan grinned.

Luke reached into a pocket, drew forth a fold of currency. Handing it to Dan, he said: 'My five hundred. Reckon you'd better be the banker. With that wad I might find it tough to pass up a poker game.'

Dan laughed, added the bills to his money belt. 'Not sure what the tab on expenses will be yet. Paying off when we take delivery. I figure we'll be in good shape.'

'With you running things, I'm sure of it,' Shofner said, then smiled broadly. 'Got a little surprise for you, partner.'

'Surprise?'

'A real humdinger! Come on up to my room.'

Luke spun on his heel, stifling Reneger's questions with a raised hand. Mounting the stairs, he led the way down the hall to a door at the end. Halting, he knocked lightly on the panel, then pushed it open.

A girl—eighteen, certainly no more than nineteen—standing at the window looking down on the street, turned. She was small, well built, and had light hair and dark eyes. In the lamplight, Dan could not tell if they were deep blue or brown.

'My wife—Della. She'll be going with us,' Luke said.

Reneger's long shape stiffened. 'Your wife!' he echoed.

Shofner beamed. 'Maybe I ought to be calling her my bride,' he said, crossing the room and placing his arm around the girl's slim waist. 'Only been married a couple of weeks.'

Della Shofner extended her hand gravely,

a slight frown on her face. Dan took it without comment. Anger had begun to burn away the surprise that had flooded him. He stirred impatiently.

'Why? I don't see—'

'Was this way,' Luke broke in, mistaking the intent of Dan's question. 'Me and Della sort of grew up together back in Kansas. Her pa's place was next to ours. Guess we always was sweet on each other.

'Then I pulled out for a look-see at the big, wide world. When I went back to do my visiting, there she was, still waiting... And changed aplenty!' he added, taking a step aside and sweeping Della's figure with an appreciative eye. 'So we up and got married.'

Dan was silent for several moments. 'And you want to bring her along,' he said finally, striving to keep the sharpness from his tone.

'You bet! She'll be mighty good to have around—do the cooking and cleaning, looking after things.'

Reneger shook his head. 'Mustanger's camp's no place for a woman, Luke. You know that. Hard living—hard on a man, worse on a woman. Best thing you can do is fix her up a place here in town to stay.'

'Not on your life!' Shofner said, continuing to smile. 'She's coming with me. I ain't letting her out of my sight—no, sir!'

Reneger scowled, stared at the floor. Luke was a damned fool to get himself into such a bind. Marrying was all right—he couldn't have cared less about that part of it—but Luke should have waited at least until they had gotten under way, had time enough to turn a camp into a halfway permanent ranch with decent living accommodations.

Hell, they didn't even know for certain they'd be staying in the Red Butte country! If the herds were few or small, or somebody else was there ahead of them, they'd be forced to move on, hunt for better areas—and dragging a woman across the ragged land they'd be up against would be pure hell. Besides, there was the Apache danger; it would set up a worry in both their minds when they were absent from camp.

'It's a mistake, Luke,' he said slowly. 'I don't like it.'

Della Shofner, bristling, eyes bright with anger, was suddenly before him. 'I'm sorry you feel that way,' she said stiffly. 'I'd hoped we'd be friends. Luke's told me so much about you that I've been looking forward to this moment. But if we can't—'

'Who says you can't?' Luke demanded, smilingly. 'Ain't no law against it.'

'Not that,' Reneger said quietly. 'Got nothing against the lady. Fact is, I figure you made a mighty fine choice—got better than you deserve. It's just that there's no place for her—or any woman—in a deal like ours.'

'I'd do my share,' Della said, eyes glowing.

46

'And I'd hold up my end in other ways, too.'

'She sure can,' Shofner declared. 'Rides like a Comanche—and shoot? She can handle a rifle with the best of them ... We'll be short on help. Said so yourself.'

Dan could not deny that. Two men trapping horses would have their work cut out for them. But he'd figured to remedy that as soon as they sold off some of their first herd. They'd have capital then and could afford to hire a couple of riders.

'Afraid your wife wouldn't be much use there.'

'You might get surprised,' Della snapped.

Reneger gave her a brief glance, turned, walked slowly across the room to the window. Drawing back the curtain, he stared out into the night. Dissatisfaction and disappointment gripped him. No woman could fit into the scheme he had devised—one that called for constant work, day and night—regardless of how able she might be. The hardships, the dangers, and the simple, bald fact of distraction insofar as Luke was concerned were all major factors that would evoke difficulties impossible to cope with. And they would have other problems in large amounts. He shrugged wearily.

'You should have waited, Luke. I'm sorry you did it.'

'No need to be,' Shofner said cheerfully.

'Della'll be my lookout, if that's what's eating you. Be no worry of yours.'

'Anything connected with the ranch we're hoping to build is my worry. Not saying you wouldn't look after her; it's not so much that. It's just that having a woman around's not good—'

'There's the real reason!' Della's head was back, and fire blazed in her eyes. 'It's not whether I'm able to do a day's work right alongside you—it's simply because I'm a woman!'

'And what a woman!' Luke Shofner said irrelevantly, again putting his arm around her.

Della shook him off irritably and took a step nearer to Reneger. 'You're one of those who thinks a woman's good for nothing except to stay home, cook, clean—have babies—wait on you hand and foot! Well, you're wrong, Mr. Reneger! I can do—'

'I think,' Dan cut in coldly, turning to Luke, 'we'd best call the deal off—forget it.' Reaching inside his shirt, he produced the fold of currency Shofner had given him as his share in the partnership. 'Here—'

'Now hold on!' Luke exclaimed, the smile finally vanishing from his lips. 'No need for you getting all riled up. Hell, I figured you'd be glad I was bringing Della along, have somebody to cook, help out around camp. Never thought you'd feel the way you do.'

'Don't give me that!' Reneger snapped. 'You're smart enough to know it'd mean problems.'

'Problems?'

'You know what I mean—and we'll have trouble enough. Here's your money.'

Shofner pulled back, angered for the first time. 'Hell, no, we're not busting this thing up! We're going right ahead, same as we planned. I've got as much to say in this as you, Dan, and don't forget it. Della's coming—'

'No—'

'I'll make you a proposition; let her stay two weeks. If things don't work out right, I'll bring her back to town, and she can live here until we get a proper ranch built. That sound all right?'

Reneger again faced the night beyond the window. The street below was quiet, only the Nugget and two or three other saloons were open. Frisco Springs's business houses closed early, he noted absently as he weighed Luke's proposal.

He reckoned he shouldn't be so obstinate, that he should give the girl a fair chance. Maybe there were exceptions to the usual—and he had made a deal with Venn for a horse and pack mules, had placed the order for grub and equipment ... He guessed he ought to give it a try.

'All right, two weeks,' he said, grudgingly.

Shofner's face lit up, and his lips parted in a wide smile. 'You won't be sorry!' he said, sticking out his hand. 'We'll prove that to him, won't we, honey?'

Della's manner was cool. 'I'm not sure I care to go,' she said. 'And I wouldn't—only I think Mr. Reneger needs to have his eyes opened. That'll be the one reason why I'll do it—prove him wrong.'

Dan shrugged. If that was the way she wanted it, so be it. He'd survive.

Luke slapped him solidly across the back, all smiles again as he tried to bridge the awkward, tight moment.

'Mr. Reneger!' he chided Della. 'Why're you calling him that? Name's Dan. No point in being so fancy about it. He's our partner—same as family!'

Della turned away and sat down on the edge of the bed. Dan crossed to the door, paused hand on the knob.

'You got horses?'

'Sure have,' Luke replied. 'Rode in from Kansas.'

'Any reason why we can't pull out tomorrow?'

'None at all. Sooner the better, I say.'

Reneger bobbed his head curtly. 'Meet you at Venn's livery stable, seven o'clock. We'll start loading the mules. Ought to be in shape to leave by noon.'

'I'll be there—partner ... Good night.'

Reneger wheeled, and stepping into the hallway, walked quickly to his room.

CHAPTER SEVEN

When Luke Shofner finally arrived at Venn's stable that next morning, nearer nine o'clock than seven, Reneger already had the pack saddles fitted to the mules and was beginning to stow the supplies he had carried from Lavendar's store.

Apologetic, Luke grinned, said: 'Reckon I must've sort of slept in ... Expect you understand. What'll I do?'

'Load,' Dan said with no particular heat. This was the way it would be, he knew, but he'd made an agreement, and he'd stand by his word. 'Bring your gear?'

'All here,' Luke answered, pointing at two saddles straddling a rack in the first stall. 'Della'll have a little bag she carries her doodads in. Can hang it on the horn. How many mules we got?'

'Four.'

'Think that'll be enough?' Luke wondered, squatting on his heels.

Reneger nodded. 'Will be, unless you've got more stuff than's in those saddlebags. How about blankets?'

'Forgot them ... They won't take up

51

much room. Can tie them onto the saddle, too. Me and Della traveled light. You still got that grulla you was riding back in Texas?'

'Sold him. Bought myself that bay over there after I got here. How about your horses? Be plenty rough going up there in the Buttes.'

'Picked up a sorrel back in Wichita. He'll do plenty good. Got Della a fine little black. Ain't fast, but he's tough. We taking along any extras?'

Reneger, working steadily and methodically to get the gear packed on the mules, shook his head. 'We can make it without a remuda for a while. Don't like spending the money.'

'Why not? With a thousand dollars—'

'Don't know for certain what we'll be up against. Bound to lose some gear, get it tore up—and that'll call for buying more. Too, we may find the Buttes no good, have to move on. Best we go slow at first.'

Luke turned to a pile of supplies and began to load one of the mules. He was a good hand at it, just as he was with most everything he undertook.

'Still think we can get away by noon?' he asked. 'Sure would make Della happy. She's mighty anxious to get going.' Luke paused, stared at Reneger. 'Sort of grieves me, Dan. Wish't you liked her better.'

Dan shook his head impatiently. 'Not a

matter of liking her. Seems a real fine girl. Just that I don't figure there's a place for her in a mustanger camp. Too hard, too rough—and she'll be seeing things no woman should. Besides—'

Shofner looked up, faced Reneger. 'Besides?' he prompted.

'Somehow, a woman always seems to put a damper on a man, hold him back—'

'Not Della!' Luke broke in. 'You'll find out she's different. She ain't the kind that'll do things or say things—and she won't mind our talking like we always do.'

Dan said, 'Could be,' in a wooden voice. There was no conviction in the words.

'You know what, Dan?' Shofner continued. 'You ought to find yourself a pretty gal, marry up with her. Then you'd have somebody to do your cooking, mend your socks, and crawl into bed with when you took the notion. Mighty pleasurable thing, that.'

Reneger shrugged. 'Ever I find a woman I want to marry, it won't be for those reasons. It'll be because I want her to share my life with me.'

'Same thing,' Luke said defensively.

Dan smiled. 'Maybe so ... guess it's all in the way you look at it. For me—'

Shadows striking suddenly across the floor just within the stable's entrance checked Reneger's words. He looked up. Trask and

Cal Hovendon, appearing tired and dusty, stood before them. He felt the lawman's hostile glance rake him, slide on to settle upon Luke.

'Want to ask you some questions, Shofner.'

Luke took a final hitch in the rope with which he was lashing down a part of the mule's burden, smiled, and stepped forward.

'Sure, Marshal. What can I do for you?'

Hovendon said: 'Like to know where you were—'

'Never mind,' the lawman cut in crisply, touching the cattleman with an irritated glance. 'I'll do the talking.' Crossing his arms, he stared at Luke. 'You know anything about a stage holdup?'

Reneger leaned against the wall of the stable's runway. 'I take it your posse didn't have much luck.'

'Found the owlhoot's horse—and figured we had the man, but we had to turn him loose,' Hovendon said, and then fell silent again as Trask whirled upon him.

'Goddammit—keep your lip buttoned up!'

The rancher flushed, looked away. Emil Trask came back to Luke. 'What about it?'

'The holdup? Sure I heard about it. Some gent got away with a pile of money. What's it got to do with me?'

'Aiming to find out. Nobody knows who you are, where you come from. You show up

54

here—then we have a holdup. Got me wondering.'

Shofner laughed. 'You thinking I had something to do with it?'

'Asking questions, that's all,' Trask replied coolly. 'What brought you here in the first place?'

'Why, my partner,' Luke said, jerking his thumb at Dan. 'We set it up to meet here.'

Hovendon looked at Reneger. 'He the partner you were talking about?'

Dan said, 'That's him.'

Emil Trask stirred. 'Seems a little pat to me—all cut and dried.'

'Sure it is. We took better'n six months getting the thing set up—while we were working on another job.'

'And it just happened the both of you landed here at the same time we had a holdup—one of you on the stage, in fact.'

There was a fine note of scorn in the lawman's tone.

Temper began to simmer within Dan Reneger once again. He drew himself up slowly.

'It just happened, Marshal,' he said lazily, echoing the lawman's own words. 'Seems to me you spend a lot of time talking to the wrong people. Luke didn't have any more to do with that robbery than I did.'

'Maybe,' Trask said indifferently. He studied Shofner quietly. 'You ain't got around to answering the first question.'

'What question?'

'Where you were yesterday morning.'

'Right here in town—at the hotel most of the time. My wife'll tell you that. Expect the hotel clerk can, too, if he's got a memory and you're of a mind to ask.'

'I'm of a mind,' Trask said, and gave the mules a calculating look. 'Pulling out?'

'Noon,' Reneger said, the word a challenge. 'Any reason we shouldn't?'

Trask crossed his arms. 'Suit yourself.'

Cal Hovendon's face registered surprise. 'But you said—'

'Know what I said,' the Marshal snapped. 'Just you keep your nose out of my business. Things'll work out fine.'

Reneger relaxed. He had half expected trouble when the lawman discovered he planned to leave town. Something had happened to make him change his thinking—or a different idea was brewing in the man's mind. And, too, he could be wrong about Emil Trask, he guessed. He could be misjudging him. He had to admit his feelings toward all lawmen were somewhat biased.

'I want you, I know where to find you,' Trask said, and then with a bleak smile added, 'Something else, Reneger—I know who you are. Thought you looked familiar, so I thumbed through the wanted dodgers I got back in my office. Come across the one that Texas judge—Patterson—had put out on you. I know just where you stand.'

Dan's muscles tensed. 'Meaning what?'

'You're walking on thin ice far as I'm concerned. You give me one reason, and I'll crack down on that probation thing Patterson's hung on you and turn you over to him so fast you'll be wondering—'

'You won't ever get the chance,' Reneger broke in. 'Not you, not anybody.'

'Things can be arranged,' the Marshal said smugly. 'Just the way you talk to a man makes it plenty easy.'

'Got nothing to do with it. Whole thing concerns me breaking the law—something I haven't done and don't intend to do.'

Trask stared at Dan from unblinking, round eyes. 'Like I said, things can be arranged. Just you watch—'

'Glad we got everything all settled,' Luke Shofner interrupted cheerfully. 'Now, what say we all go over to the Nugget, have ourselves a drink? Me and my partner'll stand treat, Marshal.'

Refusal sprang to Dan Reneger's lips. Luke was trying to head things off, smooth over a bad minute, and he appreciated the effort; but he'd have no drink with Emil Trask, not under any circumstances.

'No need,' the lawman said, relieving Dan of the necessity for denial. Abruptly, he wheeled, headed back into the street, with Hovendon a step behind him.

'Reckon the Marshal don't favor drinking with us outlaws' Luke said, grinning. 'Didn't know he figured you had something to do with that holdup.'

'Got the idea I was working with the bandit because I wasn't robbed, too. Same as accused me of being in cahoots with him.''

Luke's face sobered. 'He's a tough sonofabitch, can see that. Thought for a minute there things was going to be like old times, with the two of you tangling right smart. Real proud of the way you held back.'

Dan snugged down a coil of rope. 'Had to. Not letting anything get in the way of our plans.'

'Not even my wife?' Luke asked, making a great show of surprise.

'Not even your wife—for two weeks, anyway,' Dan answered with a slow grin. He hesitated, his gaze reaching through the wide doorway to the figures of Trask and Cal Hovendon turning into the jail.

He was putting no trust in the lawman. Trask had been too agreeable about his leaving. There was something wrong—he had something in mind ... Still, the Marshal had no grounds for holding him—much less Luke. He couldn't stop them if they wanted to leave—legally, anyway; but Dan Reneger had brushed up against the law often enough to know legal grounds weren't always a factor in a lawman's decision. Spite, prejudice, and plain, ordinary meanness were only too frequently a basis for action.

He shrugged. The hell with it. He wasn't going to worry over it. Glancing at Luke, he bent over the last pile of equipment.

'Shake loose—let's get this chore done. That drink you mentioned sounds mighty good.'

CHAPTER EIGHT

Della Shofner closed the door behind Luke. Arms at her sides, she leaned against the nearby wall. He was on his way to meet Dan Reneger—more than an hour late. She'd tried to persuade him to leave earlier but to no avail. It would be all right with Dan if he were a bit tardy, Luke had assured her; Dan would understand, but she was not so positive.

She'd be blamed for it, she supposed, and shrugged indifferently. Dan Reneger didn't like her much, that was plain, and she regretted it. She'd liked him even before they'd met. Luke had done a lot of talking about him, and she had become almost as excited over meeting him as she had at the prospect of going west with Luke after their wedding. But it hadn't worked out at all the way she had hoped.

It wasn't that he disliked her as a woman; quite the contrary, in fact. There had been that fleeting moment when she had seen the flicker of admiration in his eyes when he looked at her for the first time, had known that she stirred him strongly. No, it was simply because she *was* a woman, and to his way of thinking, there was no place for her in his plans.

Well, if it was war Dan Reneger wanted, it was war Dan Reneger would get. She'd prove to him he was wrong about her, and before those ridiculous two weeks were over, he'd be glad she was around. And she'd make him admit it, say it in plain words.

Moving away from the door, she crossed to the bed. They wanted to leave by noon, she recalled. She'd best be ready, not be the cause of any delay. Taking a small, pouch-type carpetbag from the table, she opened it and began to fold and place within articles of night clothing and other odds and ends. Dan Reneger would find no reason to complain about her being tardy.

His appearance had surprised her. From what Luke had told her of his past, she had expected Dan to be a hard-faced, grim man with little to say and a chip perpetually balanced on his shoulder. Perhaps the chip was there all right, but none of her other impressions was necessarily true.

To be told he was a killer was a little hard to accept, but she guessed it was true enough. Luke would have no reason to lie about it ... Two men, he'd said ... Both in fair fights. The last one had gotten him into bad trouble with the law. It had been one of those saloon brawls, and the victim was the son of some judge. She couldn't remember the name ... Peters or Potter ... or maybe it was Patterson.

Anyway, Dan had killed the son, and the judge had really gotten up in arms about it, even though a U.S. marshal had backed Dan and other witnesses in swearing that it was unavoidable. But Dan's past record had gone against him. He'd always been a little wild, in one scrape after another, and the judge had used that as a reason for putting him on something called probation.

He'd notified all lawmen in the surrounding states and territories to be on the watch for Dan, arrest him for the slightest thing—just so it amounted to breaking the law. All he wanted was Dan to be brought up before him on a clear charge to which he'd have to plead guilty, and then he'd sentence him to a term in the penitentiary. In that way, Luke explained, the judge would take his revenge. He couldn't put Dan away for killing his boy, so he'd use some other reason.

It wasn't a fair deal, Luke claimed, and she agreed. Dan didn't deserve to have that kind of threat hanging over his head, but the judge was big and powerful enough to make it stick. As a result, Reneger was like a man walking on eggs. But he never spoke of it. He simply took his medicine and made the best of it ... How did Luke put it? *The judge dealt him a busted flush, but he was staying in there, playing out the hand.*

That had happened almost a year ago, and Dan evidently had been able to keep himself out of trouble. It must be hard, Della thought, for a man like Dan Reneger to live carefully, avoid the things he once gloried in. He was not the sort to ever back away from anything, and being compelled to—knowing all lawmen were his enemies—must really be a strain.

The bag was packed. She snapped the brass clips, placed it in the center of the bed, and moved to the streaky mirror hanging over the chest serving as a dresser. Pausing, she studied her reflection; what did Dan Reneger truly think of her?

Not that it mattered—she didn't actually give a rap, but, well, she was curious. Luke had thought her pretty, had told her she had the best figure he'd ever seen—and he'd seen plenty ... She guessed she did have a nice shape, guessed also that was one of the things that made Luke take note of her when he returned to visit his folks.

What he'd told Dan about them wasn't exactly true. Oh, they'd lived on adjoining farms, all right, but Luke had scarcely known she existed, although, as a youngster, she imagined she had a fancy for him.

It was when he had come home and she had happened to drop by the Shofner place to deliver sewing her mother had done for Luke's mother that he had perked up. From then on, it was a whirlwind affair, and almost before she could catch her breath, she was Mrs. Luke Shofner and heading west for a town of which she'd never heard to meet a man of whom she'd heard too much.

On several occasions since, she'd had time to think about it, wonder if she really were in love with Luke or just with the idea. It was difficult to separate the two, and at each opportunity, she had passed it off, unwilling, possibly even afraid, to face the truth.

It was too late to do anything about it now, anyway, and besides, it was better than rusting away as an old maid on a Kansas farm or being married, finally and frantically, to some clumsy footed, red-neck farmer.

Actually, she should be thankful that Luke had made his visit. He'd rescued her from those probabilities, and while she, perhaps, wasn't in too great a danger of becoming an old maid—she'd turn eighteen her next birthday—there was no sense in waiting, taking a chance.

Her father hadn't liked the idea of her marrying Luke much, saying she was too young and pointed out the absence of any need for haste. Her mother had seen it her way. *If he's who you want, marry him,* she'd said, and Della had done just that. Maybe she was young, but certainly she was no child bride. Plenty of her girlfriends had married younger, some already having growing families.

She hoped she could avoid that for a while—at least until Luke and Dan got settled where they wanted to be and had the makings of a ranch under way. Babies should have a good roof over their heads and not a canvas ceiling or the open sky.

That's the way Dan Reneger would look at it, she guessed, and then wondered why it had occurred to her to think of him in such a matter. Luke would pass it off, as she had learned he was inclined to do when faced with a problem or a serious decision of some sort. He'd consider it purely her affair, not his, and depend upon her to see that it never came to pass. But if it did, she supposed it would be all right with him.

Turning from the dresser, she moved to the window and glanced out. Now that she was ready, she wished they would come. She looked down at her riding skirt, made for her by her mother. It was of heavy twill, divided so that she could sit astride a horse in comfort yet appear to be wearing the usual ladies' garment when walking.

Her shirtwaist was of twill, also, only of lighter weight and trimmed at the collar with an edging of lace to retain a trace of femininity. Luke had bought new boots for her—soft, black leather that came almost to her knees—for protection in the brush.

Her hat was something else, and thinking of it brought a smile to her lips. It was old, a castoff of her father's; stained by rain and sun, it had a misshapen, floppy brim, but it was comfortable, and she had a feeling for it. When Luke had offered to buy her a new one, she had declined ... The skirt and shirtwaist made by her mother, a hat once worn by father—somehow they made home seem less remote.

Della's vagrant thoughts came to a stop. Down the street, she saw Luke and Dan Reneger emerge from the Nugget Saloon and pause on the porch. Luke was telling Dan something, laughing as he spoke. Reneger was smiling in a quiet, withdrawn way.

He was actually nice-looking when he smiled. His eyes—gray weren't they?—sort of squeezed together, and the straight lines of his face melted. He was taller than she remembered from the night before, had thick shoulders; and the way he walked; she recalled that from the previous night, too—that slightly bent, quick, purposeful manner, as if he had to get somewhere in a hurry and God Almighty Himself wasn't going to stop him.

At that moment, the two men parted, Reneger heading for the stable at the end of the street, Luke angling, in his easygoing way, for the hotel. Thoughtful, Della pulled back from the window. Taking up her hat, she stood in front of the mirror, drew it on, pinning it securely so that it would not come off in the wind. Then laying her jacket on top of the carpetbag, she sat down on the bed. She was ready.

CHAPTER NINE

For the first few miles west of the settlement, they rode abreast with the mules trotting doggedly behind. It was open country, covered with stubby, sun-baked grass, scarred now and then with small, flinty meadows. Globular snakeweed, clumps of rabbit brush, and patches of purple loco broke the monotony at times. It was not long, however, before they reached the tumbled masses of rock that marked the beginning of the mountains.

A coolness had settled over Dan Reneger

66

when they met at Venn's and began the ride. Not a conscious retreat as such, but immediately, he had felt the outside of the trio, and as they pressed on, he heard only vaguely the words, mostly banter, exchanged by Della and Luke.

But he could not deny his admiration for the girl. She carried herself well, sat the black as one who knew and trusted horses. She made a fetching picture—a battered, old hat perched high on her head, a snowy white shirt and sensible split skirt, boots that came to her knees ... Likely she was all Luke claimed her to be—but that changed nothing.

They turned north at the foot of the mountain, searched a full mile before they found the trail, and began the ascent. It was a narrow path, hemmed in by rock and brush. At once, they were forced into single file.

'Take the lead,' Dan said, halting and motioning to Luke. 'I'll stay back of the mules. Don't want one straying.'

'Yes, sir, Colonel!' Shofner said with a flourish. And then sweeping off his hat, he inclined his head to Della. 'After you, my lady!'

Della laughed, pulled to the fore of the slowly forming column. Shofner, glancing to the sun directly above them, brushed at the sweat on his brow.

'Going to be like this all the way.'

'Won't be too bad once we're on top,' Dan said.

Luke studied the trail. 'We'll have one hell of a time bringing a herd of horses through here. You think of that?'

Reneger nodded. 'Once we get camp established, we'll locate a better trail. Ought to be one south of here, one that'll stick to the flats, skirt the mountain.'

'Wish we were on it now,' Luke said with a deep sigh.

Reneger frowned. 'Have a bad night?'

Shofner half turned, grinned. 'Nope, had a good night,' he said and winked broadly. 'But I sure could use some sleep.'

Dan settled back. Shofner spurred his sorrel, hurried to overtake Della, and then one by one, the mules, trained in such matters, singled out and began their stolid plodding up the rocky incline. When the last had gone by, Reneger swung the tall bay into the defile and followed.

A fine dust haze began to lift, hang to the side of the mountain, unmoving in the breathless air. Lizards panted in the shade of overreaching ledges, and high above, a scatter of broad-winged buzzards soared in effortless circles as they searched the hushed, steaming land for carrion.

The party gained the crest near midafternoon, and they found themselves on a lengthy, tree-covered saddle rich with deep grass. Dan, topping out last, found Shofner off his sorrel, resting in the shade.

'What say we camp here for the night, finish off in the morning while it's cool?'

Reneger pointed to a line of bluffs several miles to the northwest. 'Trail ends there. Can make it by dark.'

Luke shifted wearily. 'What's the hurry? Ride's been tough on the horses . . . And my wife.'

Dan swung down. 'Few minutes will take care of them,' he said. He glanced to Della, still astride her black. It was Luke who needed to stop, not her, he realized.

'It all right with you if we keep going?'

Della moved her shoulders slightly. 'Makes no difference to me.'

'Then we keep going,' Reneger said. 'We'll give the horses and mules a half hour.'

Shofner flung away the twig he was breaking between his fingers, rose to his feet. Striding to the sorrel, he took a bottle from his saddlebags and helped himself to a drink, ignoring Dan completely. After a moment, he glanced to Della.

'Better get off that nag, let him rest,' he said. 'Don't know what all the damned hurry's about.'

'No point wasting daylight,' Reneger stated quietly, and turned to checking the mule packs.

When the time was up, they mounted silently, resumed the trek, aiming northwest now toward the sentinel-like buttes glowing dull red beyond a green-capped ridge that trailed off indefinitely to their right. Dan rode apart from Della and Luke, again staying with the mules, although there was little danger here of straying. Traveling was easy as the climb was slight and the ground smooth.

Shofner slept, Dan noted and took relief from that. Luke was tired, irritable; he'd feel better after a nap. He grinned wryly. So far, their first day of partnership had not gone too well—but such was to be expected, he supposed, glancing at Della.

He continued to watch her. She rode easy, seemingly untouched by the hours she'd been on the black. Her features were serene, and if weariness was beginning to claim her, she gave no indication ... Della Shofner was quite a woman; he had to admit that.

The long saddle began to play out, the country to grow rougher and spattered with huge boulders. They reached the ridge, crossed, began a gradual descent toward a wild land lying well below the general plain and checkered with buttes.

Shofner awoke, scrubbed at his face, again fished the bottle of liquor from his saddlebags and had his drink. Dan watched him tuck the liquor back into its place,

70

wondered at how the man could be so different from what he had thought—wondered also if he had ever really known Luke Shofner.

But things would change. Luke was having an off day. He wasn't himself ... Tomorrow would be better ... *Tomorrow had better be,* Dan thought as they pressed on steadily.

Near dark, they reached the edge of the mesa across which they traveled and halted to look directly down into the vast sink. It was much more rugged country than it had appeared earlier; a savage, broken world of many buttes, canyons, bald knobs, and flat ledges. Heat-scoured brush grayed the slopes, and the sandy washes, catching the last of the setting sun's colors, glittered like pulverized jewels.

To their right, a dark, winnowing strip of green marked the course of a stream which originated apparently in a pine-clad profusion of higher hill rising in the north. Other clusters of trees, varying in the depth of their color, indicated additional springs either too small to create flowing creeks or else, as if discouraged by the blistering sun, turned quickly back underground.

'Partner, you sure picked the right place,' Luke, once again his genial self, observed. 'This country was made for mustangs ... Where you figure to set up camp?'

Reneger pointed to a clearing far below

and near the stream. 'Good spot there—leastwise for a spell.'

Shofner nodded, and then hesitating, frowned. 'You don't aim to stay put once we locate?'

Dan was certain he'd mentioned the possibility earlier, but he said: 'We'll have to move on if the herds aren't here. Last time through, I saw quite a bunch in the canyons and on the benches. But if they're not here now, nothing we can do but drift around until we find them.'

'I'm betting they're still here,' Luke said. 'Any horse with a lick of sense wouldn't leave this place.'

'What I'm hoping,' Reneger said, and started the mules toward the trail.

Shofner, with Della, pushed ahead, and the steep descent into the sink began. The path was badly washed out in places by the infrequent but violent rainstorms that lashed the country, and several times they were forced to halt, cut back, and find a negotiable route. But eventually, they reached the bottom and soon were halting in the small meadow near the creek.

When they dismounted, Della immediately turned to Shofner. 'Get the food unloaded. I'll fix something to eat.'

Luke grinned, wagged his head. 'Yes'm,' he said, and watched her wheel away and busy herself at collecting stones for a fire bin.

She had a meal of warmed-over meat, cornbread, fried potatoes, and coffee ready by the time they had erected one of the tents and had the horses and mules picketed for the night. Both paused at their work when she called, Reneger frankly surprised, Luke Shofner beaming.

'What'd I tell you? She's going to be a big help. Got to admit that.'

Dan nodded. He had no complaints. Della had proved herself on the hard ride from Frisco Springs and again in camp ... But this was only the first day.

CHAPTER TEN

Reneger rolled out of his blankets at daylight, found Della up before him. Hurrying to the stream, he doused his head in the icy water to clear away the cobwebs of fatigued slumber and returned to camp. Luke was stirring about by then.

Sober-faced, Della handed each a cup of steaming coffee, said: 'Breakfast's ready in a few minutes.'

The two men hunkered near the fire. The morning was chill, and a light breeze blowing in from the peaks made the warmth from the flames a welcome thing.

'What's first on the list?' Luke asked,

passing Dan his bottle of liquor.

Reneger poured a small quantity of whiskey into his coffee and returned it. 'Look the hills over, see if the herds are still around.'

Shofner sloshed his drink back and forth. 'You figure there'll be more than one bunch? Thought a stallion usually kept them rounded up in a single herd.'

'It'll be that way if there aren't many and grass is scarce. Saw three different bunches here before.'

Luke stared off into the brightening landscape, shot now with reflected yellows and golds. The buttes appeared blood red in the predawn glow.

'Figure it'd be smart if you'd have a quick look-see soon as you're done with your vittles ... I'll hang around camp, start sorting things out, getting set.'

Dan nodded. 'If that's how you want it.'

'Not much sense in me going—you're the one who knows all about trapping. Save time if I was to work on the camp.'

Della, still grave and silent, moved up, bringing plates for each heaped with bacon, fried mush cakes, and biscuits loaded with honey. Reneger thanked her quietly, and she smiled, breaking the reserve of her soft features. She looked very young and fresh in the early light; her eyes, he noted, were actually a deep blue, near violet.

'More coffee?'

At her question, he held out his cup. Shofner reached for the whiskey bottle, which, unlike the previous day, he evidently was of a mind to share. Dan shook his head. He was not particularly fond of liquor in his coffee but simply found it a good idea when cold bit deep into his bones. Coffee was coffee, whiskey was something else; he preferred to take them separately.

'That be all right with you—me staying in camp?' Luke pressed.

There was no object in setting up a base to any great extent until they were certain they had chosen the right location—something that could be determined only by the availability of the wild horse herds, but Dan made no issue of it. That Luke was in no mood for a hard, hot ride was evident.

It didn't matter. He could do much better scouting alone—but things would have to change. Luke must assume his responsibilities if they were to make a go of the venture. At the first opportunity, when they were alone, he'd make that clear.

'Suits me,' he said, feeling Della's eyes upon him, wondering, questioning. It would seem she was not in agreement with Luke's suggestion. 'Ought to be back around noon or thereabouts.'

Finishing his meal, he arose, started for the creek to wash his dishes. Della halted him.

'I'll do that.'

Reneger surrendered his utensils, thanked her in a polite, impersonal way, and moved to where the horses were picketed. Saddling the bay, he checked his canteen, looked to the rifle in its boot, and mounting, swung toward the first of the rock benches a quarter mile to the west. When he reached the first rise on the opposite side of the creek, he glanced back. Luke was still sprawled by the fire, cup in one hand, bottle in the other.

He guessed he should have insisted Luke accompany him. He could have pointed out the natural traps they might make use of, acquainted him with some of the tricks and methods he had learned that would enable them to bring in mustangs without too much difficulty.

But he hadn't, and somehow it didn't matter—and that wasn't good. The job would require both of them. In reality, a half dozen men working at it wouldn't be too many—and now with Luke hanging back, shirking his duties ... So far, he'd been a big disappointment, had turned into a different man from the one he had worked with and known, or thought he knew... How could he change so fast? Maybe with time—

The sun, in a flaring blaze, caught him when he was halfway to the bench. He halted, looked back over the sprawling, broken country coming alive now in muted browns, tans, grays, and sage greens. Where the stream cut its erratic course, the colors were dark, full-bodied but only paces away where no moisture reached, there was marked difference. Water was the lifeblood of this majestic, terrifying land, and the presence or absence of it was easily determined.

That fact would help considerably in trapping operations. Horses would stay within range of water. By singling out the canyons with springs and locating the particular areas where there were creeks, he and Luke would have no difficulty in choosing snare sites.

The first bunch of mustangs should come to hand with little trouble, unless there had been others hunting ahead of them. He doubted that. So far, he had seen no indication of such. The horses would become wary after the first catch, as they always did—but at least, they'd have a start.

Luke...

Thoughts of him again returned to nag and worry at Dan Reneger. Was there much point in going on with the partnership? Could he be expected to help, share the load, or would his lack of interest continue? Dan rolled the question about in his mind as the bay climbed steadily up the narrow game trail. There was money enough remaining to return Shofner's five hundred dollars, although it would leave him strapped. But he could get by, especially if they were fortunate enough to bring in a few mustangs immediately and sell them off.

Maybe he was expecting too much of Luke—a man just married and undoubtedly still in the clouds. Perhaps he would straighten up as time wore on. Reneger didn't want to be unreasonable, but if he were to carry the load alone, then there was no need for a partner. Better to hire a couple of riders with his share of the cash they'd receive from the first sale and let Shofner go his way.

Two weeks, he decided suddenly. That's what he'd allow—the same two weeks he'd agreed to having Della in camp. If Luke hadn't squared away and come through by then, the partnership would be dissolved.

Reneger halted abruptly, kneed the bay in beneath an overhang of rock. Across a wide, sandy wash, motion had caught his attention. Leaning forward, he strained to see into the shadowy depths of the grease-wood and taller brush marking the bank of the wash. After several moments, he settled back, satisfaction flowing through him.

A sleek, long-legged black horse emerged from the undergrowth. Ears perked, coat glistening in the sunlight, he walked slowly into the open, his narrow head swinging from side to side as he swept the surrounding country with alert suspicion.

Shortly, another horse came into view ... A third ... And then, a steady procession followed. A good herd! They were moving quietly, picking their way, keeping well within the brush.

Reneger frowned. 'Something's trailing them,' he muttered.

It could be a mountain lion hoping to pick off a straggler; or it could be other mustangers. Tense, Dan waited out the moments in the breathless heat pocketed under the ledge. The stallion neighed shrilly, broke into a run. At once, the others rushed to follow, flowing out of the undergrowth in an undulating wave of color as they swept across the lower end of the wash, up and over a ridge.

Four riders appeared at the point where Dan had first spotted the stallion. Dismay rolled through him. Lean, wiry men, their copper bodies gleamed in the sun as they sat motionless looking into the direction the herd had vanished.

Apaches ... Reneger swore feelingly. The Indians hunted the Red Butte country too! It was far east of their usual range, but the warriors were notorious for ignoring boundary lines, imaginary or otherwise. He gave that thought—it could be just a stray hunting party far off their usual grounds. That they did not pursue the herd could mean they were not seeking mustangs. Most Apaches preferred to steal their mounts from the ranchers, anyway.

Hopeful, he watched the quartette finally wheel, strike west toward the distant Escudilla Peaks. He sighed thankfully; only a few wandering braves—but he realized it was a fact he must know for certain. He'd best look for a camp or village. Waiting until the Indians were out of sight, he put the bay in motion, followed out the game trail to a high point where he could see far to the west.

No smoke was rising from any of the canyons. He felt better at once. He continued on, and then shortly, he saw the Apaches. They were beyond the sink, moving steadily westward. He guessed he was right; only a stray party. They'd had their look and were now retreating to home ground on the far side of the distant range of hills. Nevertheless, their presence had disturbed him, and there was the possibility they could return, bring others. In days to come, he would need to watch sharp.

At midmorning, he had climbed to the uppermost point in the sunken land, looked over mile upon mile of the surrounding country. He had seen no more Indians, was more convinced now than before that he had nothing to fear from them.

He saw two more herds, one to the north and one to the west, both smaller than the bunch led by the black. He turned then to searching for definite, well-used trails and eventually found several that led to a narrow canyon where the horses evidently watered regularly. It was an *embudo*, a narrowing, dead-end box, and to throw a gate across its lower opening would be simple, since the mouth was little more than two dozen strides in width.

They'd make their first catch there, he decided, pulling to a halt on a bald knob to fix landmarks and get his bearings. After that, he'd ferret out other trails and box canyons ... For now, this one would do.

Glancing to the sun, now past its zenith, he swung the bay toward camp. He and Luke could start early in the morning, using one of the mules to pack in the necessary rope and wire to construct a gate. It shouldn't take long to trap their first herd.

CHAPTER ELEVEN

On toward the middle of the afternoon, Dan Reneger rode into camp. He halted the bay at the picket rope beside the other animals and swung down stiffly. It had been a hot, dusty ride through the upper buttes, and he was tired and soaked with sweat.

Neither Della nor Luke were in evidence as he unsaddled the bay, and after the hull was off, he spent another ten minutes rubbing down the big horse. He was pleased with the bay. Amos Venn had sold him a good mount. Finished, he turned and walked into the camp proper. He was not particularly hungry, but the coffeepot perched on the edge of the fire bin caught his eye, and obtaining a cup, he helped himself to a measure of the lukewarm liquid.

He heard sound behind him as he settled back on his heels and glanced up. It was Della. Apparently, she and Luke had been asleep in the tent, and his coming had awakened her.

'Want something to eat?' she asked.

Dan shook his head. 'Don't bother. I'll wait for supper.'

'No bother. Will a sandwich do?'

Without waiting for his reply, she crossed to where the supplies, still in sacks and box containers, were piled on a mound of rocks and began to prepare him a snack of bread and meat. There had been little if anything done during his absence, he noted idly.

Della, bringing the sandwich and a cup for herself, returned to where he hunched. Handing him the bread and meat, she poured herself some coffee.

'Luke thought we'd be going to a lot of

work for nothing, fixing up the place if you decided we shouldn't stay here,' she said. She hadn't missed his swift assessment.

He made no reply, watching her circle the dead fire and find a place to sit on a hummock of grass. Her belligerence toward him seemed to have lessened somewhat.

'Did you see any horses?'

'Three herds.'

Interest brightened her eyes. Her lips parted to speak and then closed as Luke appeared in the tent's opening.

'Howdy ... Thought I heard talking,' he said, stretching lazily. 'Any luck?'

'Some,' Reneger replied. 'Three different bunches. One fair size—maybe forty head. Others were about half that.'

Shofner brushed at the sweat in his face, crossed to Della's side. 'How close?'

'Eight, ten miles due west.'

'Seem spooky—like there'd be somebody else around?' Luke asked, reaching for Della's hand and guiding her cup to his mouth. He took a swallow, made a wry face.

'Nothing special.'

'Figure it'll be much of a chore trapping them?'

Reneger set his empty cup aside. 'Country's plenty rough. Mostly box canyons and benches. Won't be too much work making traps. There's one canyon with a good spring in it where the horses have been watering regularly. Could make our first try.'

Luke shrugged, sprawled out on the warm ground. 'That mean we'll have to drive them into the box?'

'Two of us could never haze forty mustangs into anything. Smart thing to do is build a gate across the opening, lay back until they come in to water, then close them in.'

'We'll make this our permanent camp, then,' Della said, putting it as a statement rather than a question. She glanced about absently. 'I'm glad. I like it here.'

'Little hot, ain't it?' Luke commented.

'Maybe in the middle of the day,' Reneger said, 'but we're protected from the wind, and we're close to water. Plenty of level ground for corrals and sheds.'

He rose, eyes sweeping out across the small flat below them. 'Figure to build corrals there,' he said, pointing to a grass-covered area 100 yards distant. 'Be easy to dig a ditch, divert water from the stream into a watering pond. Back up toward—'

'Instead of building corrals, why can't we use that box canyon for a pen? Gate'd already be there—and it'd sure save a lot of work.'

Dan shook his head. 'Never handle a herd in one of those canyons, even a small one.

Probably kill more horses than we'd take out.'

'Don't see how the hell you aim to get them out of here, anyway,' Shofner said sourly. 'Driving a half broke bunch of broncs over that mountain trail—'

'Won't have to. Took a good look at the country when I was up high. Land to the south is flat. Be no problem swinging around the foot of the mountain and reaching Frisco Springs that way. Take a day or so longer, maybe, but I don't see as that'll matter ... Could even bring a wagon in, once we've smoothed out a few humps.'

'Will we build a house—a real one, I mean?' Della asked, her face glowing.

Reneger nodded. 'Plenty of timber up above us. Easy to cut what we need, skid it down the slope.' He paused, smiled at her. 'A log cabin—not a house like you're maybe thinking of.'

'Wouldn't matter. I just like to think we'll have something besides tents to live in.'

'Not sure that'd be smart,' Luke said, reaching for his cigarette makings. 'What if the herds get wise, pull out after we've made our first gather? We'd be setting here, high and dry.'

'Some might, but this is good mustang country. Looked to me like there was a lot of coming and going. Even if we scared off what's running loose now, other bunches will drift in. They remember where the water holes are and where grazing's good.'

'Could run into a lot of time—just setting around, waiting on herds to drift in.'

'Be a good thing,' Dan said. 'We'll need time once we've got a corral full of wild broncs to tame. I figure it ought to work out about right.'

Luke stared off toward distant, towering Spur Peak, rising like a white-capped volcano above the green slopes of the lesser mountains. Della leaned forward, her expression eager.

'How soon can we start?'

'The cabin?' Dan said, smiling at her. 'Afraid it'll have to be about the last thing in the list. Plenty of good weather ahead before we'll need it, anyway. Tents will do fine for a while.

'First thing we've got to do is get some gates hung at the canyons where I spotted water, then let things ride a few days so's the horses will get used to the change. Old stallion leading that big bunch has plenty of savvy. Be hard to fool him.

'Once we've hung gates, we'll get busy on the corrals. That'll be the biggest job, because it'll take a strong, high fence. These mustangs can jump higher than you think. After that, we're set for business and can start building a good camp. We'll need a fair-sized cabin, one we can split into several rooms—'

'Be nice to have the kitchen off the back with a door leading into the house so's we can close it during hot weather, leave it open in winter,' Della said.

'Good idea,' Dan agreed. 'We'll need a barn of sorts, too; place where we can keep our working stock in out of the weather, store feed and gear...'

'A cellar would be a good thing,' Della continued. 'Ought to have a cool place to put food, keep it so's we'll have it for later.' She glanced around. 'Would a garden grow here? I could get seeds, plant things like corn and squash, and maybe cabbage and onions and such.'

'All good mountain topsoil. Should be able to grow most anything you want.'

'And if we could get a cow—have chickens—'

Dan Reneger studied the girl with renewed interest. She had really been caught up with the exciting prospects of building a home. Admiration again stirred him. He shifted his gaze to Luke, realizing suddenly that he had shown no particular interest in the planning.

'How's all this sound to you?'

Shofner plucked the dead cigarette from his lips, flipped it into the ashes of the fire.

'Count me out,' he said flatly. 'Soon as we sell off the first herd, I'm taking my share of

the cash, and then me and Della are moving
on.'

CHAPTER TWELVE

A gasp of surprise escaped Della's lips.
Reneger stared at Shofner, but strangely,
there was no shock in the man's words. Luke
had proved a different man from what he
had thought, and already, he had come to
decisions of his own as to the future of their
relationship.

'You know what you're saying?'

Shofner grinned. 'Don't I always? Hell, I
hate busting things up, but laying here, I got
to thinking, come up with some new plans.
Aim to see some of the big towns—San
Francisco, Virginia City, go on up into the
Oregon country and the like. With the stake
I'll get for my share of that big herd, I can do
it.'

Della had risen, was staring at Luke.
Concern and astonishment pulled her
features into a frown.

'I—I thought this was what you
wanted—the way you'd like to spend the rest
of your life!'

'Man can change his mind,' Shofner
replied. 'Fact is, I'm plain tired of working
like a dog all the time. I'm going to do some
loafing—and looking. Some day, maybe I'll

feel like settling down on a ranch of my own, raise cattle.'

'Going to take a fair-sized stake to do all that,' Reneger said dryly. 'Come to a lot more'n your share of the cash we'll get for that herd—if we're lucky enough to trap and sell the whole bunch.'

'Be enough. It's that big herd you aim to go after, ain't it?'

'We'll take what we get. If we're lucky, that'll be the one we'll find in the canyon when we jerk the gate.'

Dan came upright. The problem insofar as Della was concerned was settled—just as his dissatisfaction with Luke was also. He need worry no more about either. They'd trap their first herd, sell them off, and then the Shofners would be on their way. With his part of the money, he'd hire a couple of riders to help, maybe an old man to cook and look after things while he went ahead with his plans ... He guessed it would work out better.

'Still means a couple of weeks,' he said, looking off into the sink. 'Need a camp just the same.'

Shofner stirred, glanced to the sun. 'Too late to start making a gate. What do you want done around here?'

Luke sounded like a hired hand—and that's the way it would be from then on, Dan supposed. He hoped they'd have good luck and immediately trap a sufficient number of mustangs to fill Luke's needs. He disliked the idea of the situation dragging on and on.

'Better get the other tent up,' he said, and pointed to a level place beyond the fire bin. 'Put it there, move the grub and cooking gear inside, where it'll be safe and all in one spot. I'll lay my bedroll in there, too.'

Luke rose, turned away at once, strode to where the supplies were piled, and dragged the canvas fold to the designated spot. He seemed angry at himself, or perhaps it was a forced sort of patience, as if he resented the thought of having to remain even for so short a time.

'Give me a hand here, Della,' he said without looking around.

Dan watched the girl, tight-lipped and crushed, follow Luke into the clearing. After a moment, he wheeled, walked to where the horses and mules were picketed. They were too close to camp. A better place for them would be downstream.

Taking up a coil of rope, he walked to a point where he intended eventually to erect his corrals, and selecting four squat piñon trees as corner posts, proceeded to string a temporary yard. The stock would have ample grass as well as water there for a time; when the patch became overgrazed, it would be simple to move the ropes to a different location.

The horses and mules transferred, he returned to the camp. Luke and Della had the tent erected and were carrying the supplies from the rock shelf to its interior.

They'd need benches, a table of sorts for Della to prepare meals on, another for dining purposes. He removed a large square of canvas he'd ordered, thinking to put it on the ground beneath their bedrolls and thus improve sleeping comfort. It would serve better now as a canopy over the tables and prove useful in turning back the sun and shedding rain. He'd need four straight and stout poles for that and rope to form guys.

He laid the canvas to one side. It would have to wait until he had time to go above for timber of proper size. There was nothing suitable in the basin, only piñon and shaggy junipers and cedars.

A better fire bin was a more pressing need. He'd picked up three short iron bars at Venn's for just such a purpose. Taking them from the pack saddle where they had been lashed, he dropped them near the small arrangement Della had constructed for cooking use, and then moving to the foot of the slope, he began toting in larger rocks. He felt he had to keep busy.

★ ★ ★

The last of the supplies and equipment

moved into the tent, Della brushed at the beads of sweat on her forehead with the back of a hand and glanced at Dan Reneger. He was carrying stones into the center of the camp, evidently intending to build a larger and better fireplace upon which to cook.

His face was solemn, and there was a set purpose to his movements. He was going ahead with his plans for a ranch regardless of what happened, she realized. He was that way; once he'd made up his mind, set a course for himself, nothing would deter him.

'Reckon I'd better drag in some firewood,' Luke murmured at her elbow, and taking up an ax, moved on by, pointing for a mound of dead trees and brush that had been swept into a pile by some storm in the past.

She nodded, thoughtfully watched him walk away, and then wheeling, she crossed to where Reneger was beginning to fit stones into a three-sided square.

'Need more?' she asked.

He did not look up. 'Expect this is enough.'

She remained silent for several moments, listening to the hollow thunk of Luke's chopping, and then moved in nearer.

'I'm glad you're going ahead with your plans.'

Dan shrugged. 'Nothing's changed—only the partnership.'

'It's the right thing. I know how much it

means to you.'

He only nodded, continued to place the stones.

'I'm sorry about Luke changing his mind. I didn't know—had no idea.'

Reneger looked at her closely. Apparently, he had thought her to be a part of the decision.

'The way it goes,' he said, and resumed his work.

'I remember Luke telling me how much you'd wanted to start a horse ranch—were always making plans, looking for the day when you could quit working for someone else, get on your own.'

'Every man looks for something.'

There was a lost quality to his words, and Della was suddenly aware of the depth of his loneliness; he was a solitary man, one never really close to another.

'Everybody needs somebody,' she said in gentle contradiction.

'No,' he said, 'not everybody.'

He had built the walls of the fire bin to three-quarters the height he had planned and reached now for the bars lying beside him. Placing them across opposing walls to form a grill, he began to secure them by adding more flat stones.

'You're not sorry Luke's leaving?'

'Chances are it never would have worked.'

'Because of me?'

93

He faced her. 'Because of you,' he said bluntly.

Oddly, she felt neither hurt nor anger at his words, and she spent a minute wondering why. 'No reason why it couldn't,' she said finally. 'Truth is, you made up your mind about me and wouldn't change it—not even if I proved you wrong.'

He fitted the last rock into place. 'Something you'd never understand,' he said, rising. He grinned at her in a dry, sardonic way. 'Not much use talking about it now, anyway. It's done with.'

She mustered a return smile. 'I suppose not, only I'm curious. Would you have changed your mind?'

'About you?'

Della's head moved slightly. 'You were giving me two weeks—like I was on trial.'

'You were.'

'And at the end of the two weeks?'

He turned, looked off into the distance, his face clouded into a frown. Shadows were beginning to lengthen, colors were growing dull, dissolving into a sameness, and the withering heat was at last breaking.

'How the hell can I answer that?' he demanded harshly. 'Only been a couple of days.' His manner softened. 'Things happen, cause a man to see different ... I can change my mind—have done it, in fact, no matter what you think.'

94

'And you changed it about me?' Della insisted. For some reason, not understood even by her, she had to know.

He gave her an exasperated glance, started toward the stream. 'I did,' he snapped, 'not that it matters a damn now.'

A glow of satisfaction claimed Della Shofner. Smiling, she watched him stalk away, stiff and unyielding. 'Dan,' she called impulsively. 'Thanks for the fine cook stove.'

He hesitated, looked back. 'Too bad you won't get to use it for long,' he said, and continued.

*   *   *

'Best bet,' Reneger said later that night as they sat in front of the fire, 'will be to string a gate across that canyon where the spring is. Sure to get horses there quick.'

The evening meal was over, the pans and dishes cleaned and stowed away. A pot of coffee simmered on the grill of the new fire bin.

Luke, stretched before the low flames, said lazily: 'How long you figure it'll take to set a gate?'

'Day. Maybe less. Might save time if we split up the job.'

'What I like to hear,' Shofner said, lacing his cup liberally with whiskey. 'How do we do that?'

Luke seemed anxious now to be on his way sooner than the projected two weeks. Dan guessed he couldn't blame him. He'd been that way himself; once he took it in mind to do something, go somewhere, he couldn't get at it quick enough ... It was all right with him ... There was no good reason for prolonging matters any more than necessary.

'You and your wife could start making a rope and wire gate in the morning—here in camp. Be faster and easier with everything handy.'

Shofner bobbed his head. 'Then pack it in on one of the mules ... What'll you be doing—getting the herd lined up?'

'No need for that. If we make use of that canyon where the spring is, they'll drift in on their own ... I'll get up there first thing, put the corner posts in, have them ready by the time you show up with the gate. Need to take a look at the upper end of the box, too. Don't think there's a trail out, but we've got to be sure.'

'Sounds good,' Luke said with no great interest. 'How long a gate you want?'

'Thirty feet ought to do it. We can brace it with crosspieces after it's been hung.'

Luke tipped his cup and drained the last of its contents. He glanced to Della, a half smile on his lips.

'Think we can make the man a gate, doll?'

She merely nodded, kept her eyes on the fire. Luke continued to stare at her.

'You don't cotton much to us pulling out, do you?'

Della said: 'I don't understand it, that's all.'

'Why not? Anything wrong with a man wanting to go places, see things—show his wife a good time?'

'No—only—'

'Only what?'

'Well, this seems such a fine chance for us—for you. Why couldn't we stay, maybe a year, save up more money—'

'You're forgetting you ain't liable to be here two weeks from now, all depending on how the boss feels. Far as money goes, my share'll be plenty—and I can always get myself a job.'

'Punching cows? Working for some rancher at forty dollars a month? Take a long time.'

'Managed to get by up to now,' Luke said stiffly.

Della's lips formed a quick retort, but she let it go unsaid and looked away. Before Luke had only himself to think of, provide for, Dan thought; was he forgetting he now had a wife—and on a ranch hand's wages...

'I'm turning in,' Shofner said abruptly, pulling himself upright. Hesitating, he looked down at Reneger, 'Better show me just how you want that gate made before you pull out in the morning ... Sure do want to get it just right.'

Dan ignored the heavy sarcasm. 'Be glad to,' he said, tossing another handful of sticks onto the fire. 'See you—early.'

'Early,' Luke echoed, and extended his hand to Della. 'Come on.'

For a moment, she appeared to decline, and then rising, she followed Luke toward their tent. Reaching there, she slowed, looked back.

'Good night, Dan.'

Reneger nodded. It came to him then; he'd miss her when she was gone.

CHAPTER THIRTEEN

Remembering the Apaches, Dan Reneger slipped a dozen extra cartridges into his pocket that next morning. Then, with ax and spade tied to his saddle, he rode out, striking west for the canyon where the spring flowed.

Very few words had passed between him and Luke Shofner, and the barrier that had risen between them seemed to have grown more pronounced overnight. There were only a few terse instructions concerning the building of the gate and the route to follow when the job was done—and nothing more.

Della, too, had little to say, and when Dan moved off, he did so in a bitter silence.

The mood did not linger for long. Essentially a loner, Reneger had years ago learned the futility of placing too much faith and reliance in others and accepted the need for depending entirely upon himself in most matters without conscious thought. Thus, the failure of the partnership was scarcely more than a passing incident, regrettable but not wholly unexpected ... It was far from his mind shortly as he crossed the awakening land, taking as always keen enjoyment from its austere grandeur and ethereal hush.

He'd build the ranch where the camp now was; first trip into town, he'd see about filing on the property—it should be available at practically no cost at all—and then once his, he'd gradually improve his holdings until the long-sought dream was a reality.

There was something to be said for Luke's idea of trapping a herd of mustangs quick and cashing in immediately. He could use the money to get under way properly, as well as hire some help ... Best to forego his original plan for culling out the best of the horses captured, keeping them for breeding stock. He could put that into effect when he had the second bunch safely in his corrals.

Two hours later, as he was drawing near the canyon, he spotted a small herd moving toward the south and realized the horses had been in the canyon for water. His pulses quickened as he watched from the dense brush ... Twenty-seven in number ... Led by a showy white with black markings and a long, flowing tail. The horses were in excellent condition, sleek and glossy in the streaming sunlight—tribute to the fine crop of grass that carpeted the slopes as a result of a wet spring. He'd like to have that white stallion. What a stud he'd make!

The mustangs dropped from sight in a piñon grove. Only then did Dan Reneger move on, having no wish to alarm the herd by revealing his presence. He reached the mouth of the canyon, again halted ... Only one post would be needed for the gate, he saw. A twisted, thick-trunked juniper growing hard against the west wall of the entrance would serve as the other. That was luck.

First, however, he'd better have a look at the upper end of the canyon, determine if there was anything needed at that point. Swinging the bay around, he entered the slash. Keeping near the foot of the steep east slope, he began the climb, aware of the possibility of other horses being at the spring.

The canyon was a perfect trap. The deeper he moved in, the more perpendicular the walls became. There was no water in the creek bed running down its center, although there was evidence that a stream had flowed in times past—probably after heavy rains—and that was a mark in his favor. The herds would be compelled to travel the entire length of the canyon to reach the spring, thus allowing ample time to pull the gate into place and make it secure.

The spring, he found, came from beneath a rock palisade that rose to towering height and formed the end of the box. It spread into a pool some 30 feet in width, was possibly knee-deep. The surrounding grass was close cropped, and there were hundreds of hoof prints in the soft loam edging the bank. There was little doubt the spring was used often by many different herds.

Dismounting, Reneger made a careful check along the base of the palisade, finally heaved a sigh of satisfaction. There was no opening, no possible trail of any sort. Not even a man, much less a horse, could scale the sheer wall. There was nothing to be done at that end of the trap.

Returning to the bay, he rode back down the canyon, again staying as much in the brush as possible and making a minimum of noise. Several times, he frightened small cottontail rabbits into frantic escape and was continually scolded by saucy tassel-eared squirrels darting about in the trees growing on the slopes and the narrow floor of the canyon.

Once, he halted to examine a set of

mountain lion tracks imprinted clearly in the loose sand of the creek bed. The tracks were not old—a day perhaps, but certainly no more than that. Once things were under way, he'd best take time out and hunt down the killer. He wanted no big cat lurking about in the brush, frightening the herds and preying on the young colts.

Again at the mouth of the canyon, he swung down, picketed the bay in a pocket of feathery sage, and taking the spade, selected the proper spot for the east gatepost and began to dig.

The ground was hard, studded with rocks, and he spent a solid hour hollowing the opening to necessary depth. That finished, and sweating profusely, he had a drink from his canteen and sat down in the shade of a large boulder to catch his breath and rest. The stillness was absolute, and he leaned back contentedly ... This was what Dan Reneger liked—what he wanted... The vast land, the arching, blue sky, the sharp, clean heat—solitude. A man could ask for no more.

Rested, long body cooled, he rose, and this time taking the ax, moved off a short distance and felled a pine of medium size. Cutting it to a 12-foot length, he trimmed it of limbs, and then using the bay, dragged it to the posthole.

Tipping it upright by his own strength, he

filled in around it with soil and rocks, tamping all solidly into place. To further secure the post, he carried in a number of stones and banked them around the base. Testing it, he found it firm.

He glanced to the sun. The morning had fled. Luke should be arriving with the gate if he and Della had kept at their chore. It wouldn't take long to get it hung—they should be finished well before dark—and then their first trap would be ready. There was a possibility, a small one, to be sure, that they could make their initial catch the next morning.

Picking up the ax, he returned to where he had dropped the pine, finished stripping the branches, and carried them back to the mouth of the canyon. The limbs would come in handy for disguising the new post, help also to destroy any odors the mustangs might find suspicious.

Dan paused as the faint, distant sound of a gunshot flatted through the quiet. Frowning, he stared into the east. The report had come from that direction—the direction in which camp lay. Alarm lifted within him. Apaches? He wished now he'd mentioned seeing the hunting party to Luke; he had intentionally kept silent about it for Della's sake, not wishing to worry her. Now ... After a minute, he shook the thought. There had been only one shot. If it was an Indian attack, he would have heard more shooting.

He resumed his work. Likely Luke had killed a rabbit or possibly even a deer. There were quite a few of the big, long-eared mule bucks roaming the flat above camp. One could have come down for water, and Shofner, seeing the possibility of fresh meat, had downed it. Or it could have been a rattlesnake. There were plenty of those, too, basking in the rocks.

The task of collecting sufficient branches completed, Dan seized the spade and began to dig the shallow trench across the mouth of the canyon where a draw rope would be buried. Once the herd was inside the trap, the rope, attached to the saddle of a horse, would be jerked tight, pulling the gate into place quickly, holding it rigid until it could be secured to the post.

He completed that job, sat down once more in the shadow of the boulder. Where the hell was Luke? He pondered that as he scrubbed away the sweat clothing his face. It was well past noon. Shofner should have ridden in an hour or more ago.

The gunshot ... He fell to thinking of that again, considered anew its possible meaning. Could it have something to do with Luke's failure to appear? He could think of no reason other than an attack by the Apaches, and that didn't sound reasonable. But something was causing a delay ...

something.

Abruptly, Reneger got to his feet, strode to where the bay waited. Best he head back, find out what was going on. Perhaps he'd encounter Luke coming up the trail, and if so, all well and good. But if not ...

★   ★   ★

Della worked steadily beside Luke at putting the gate together, twisting the lengths of rope, binding the joints so's there'd be no sag, just as Dan Reneger had directed. The gate would have to be strong, he'd said; strong enough to withstand the lunging of a powerful horse, yet pliant enough to cause no injury.

She hesitated, brushed a wisp of hair from her eyes, watched Luke take a drink from his cup. *Coffee royal*, he called it—two-thirds coffee, one-third whiskey, only this morning, it seemed to her the proportions were being reversed.

Not that it had any outward effect upon Luke. She'd never seen him drunk, although he drank considerably. He was one of those who carried his liquor well, she guessed. In that moment, she realized suddenly that she scarcely knew Luke Shofner at all. Everything had happened so fast ... Had she been in too much of a hurry? Would it have been better to heed her father, waited, gotten better acquainted? A little late to be thinking of that now, she decided wryly.

A foreign sound interrupted her reflections. She looked up. Four men were coming down the slope, heading into camp. She frowned, glanced to Luke. He had heard them, too, was eyeing them warily.

'Who—' she began, but he silenced her with a slight motion of his hand.

'The Marshal,' he said in a low voice. 'Fat one's named Hovendon. Owns a ranch around here somewhere. Others look like deputies.'

Della got to her feet. 'What do they want with us?'

'Now, how the hell would I know?' Luke answered, also rising. Shifting his gun holster forward, he added: 'Let me do the talking.'

The men rode in close, halted near the tent. The Marshal, a big, hard-faced man with shoe-button eyes, dismounted casually. Reaching into his saddlebags, he pulled out a yellow slicker, then moved up to where he was in arm's length of Luke.

'This yours?' he asked, flinging the slicker at Luke.

Luke caught it, his face expressionless as he examined it absently. 'Could be. Had one, same as plenty other men.'

'Your name's on it,' the lawman stated quietly. 'Burned with an iron.'

'Then I reckon it belongs to me,' Luke

106

said, smiling. 'I'm obliged to you—'

'You're under arrest,' the Marshal cut in, his manner suddenly harsh. 'I'm taking you in for holdup and murder. Where's the money?'

The smile faded from Luke's face. He frowned, glanced to the men beyond the Marshal. His shoulders came forward slowly. 'Money? What money? What the hell are you talking about?'

'You know what I'm talking about!' the lawman snarled. 'Stage was held up by a man wearing this slicker. Got the hat and mask he was wearing, too. Found them right where he—you hid them. Now I want to know where you stashed that satchel!'

An abrupt change swept over Luke Shofner. A wildness flared in his eyes. He threw a desperate glance at Della, dipped suddenly as his hand swept downward for the pistol on his hip.

'You'll play hell finding it!' he shouted, drawing his weapon.

The lawman fired once, his gun coming up in a blurred, dully shining streak. Shocked, Della screamed as Luke staggered. She reached him as he fell, stood frozen for a long moment over him, stunned by the swiftness of it all. Then crouching, she took his face in her hands, knew instantly he was dead. She screamed again, sprang to her feet, and whirled on the lawman.

107

'You've killed him!' she shrilled, clawing at him like a tigress.

He knocked her aside brutally with a sweep of his arm, sent her sprawling to the ground. Leaning over Luke, he probed briefly.

'Dead,' he said, drawing to his full height. He stared at Della, black eyes cold as winter. 'All right, sister, where is it?'

The girl stirred weakly, senses still scattered and hazy from the lawman's blow. 'Where's—what?'

'The money, goddammit! The twenty thousand dollars he took off Hovendon!'

'Twenty thousand!' Della gasped, jolted into reality. 'I didn't know—don't know anything about it!'

'Was a fool thing to kill him,' Hovendon said then, stepping up beside Luke's body. 'Ought've waited.'

'Wait!' the Marshal echoed scornfully. 'In my business, you better shoot first when a man goes for his gun, do the questioning afterward.' He made a gesture at the two deputies, still on their saddles. 'Look around for that satchel.'

His attention swung to Della, now struggling to rise. Placing one booted foot on her thigh, he pinned her to the ground, and grasping a handful of her hair, he jerked savagely.

'Start talking! Where is it?'

108

Della bit back a cry of pain. 'I told you—I don't know!' she blazed.

The lawman released his grip on her hair, slapped her sharply across the face, and stepped away. 'Better be remembering!' he warned. 'I got ways of making you—'

'Ain't in here, Emil,' one of the deputies called from the tent.

'Keep at it—that ain't the only place he could've hid it,' the Marshal snapped. He turned, glared at Hovendon. 'Won't hurt none for you to help. It's your money.'

The rancher wheeled, began to poke about in the empty boxes and sacks piled near the supply tent. 'Just the same, I'm thinking it was a damn-fool stunt to kill him,' he said again.

'And it was a damn-fool stunt of yours to go shooting off your mouth in the first place,' the lawman shot back. 'Surprised you ain't been held up before.'

'Supposed to be law in this country—'

'There is—and you know it goddam well! Only yahoos like you fix it so's it'll get broke, doing a lot of blabbing and bragging.'

'Which ain't getting us nowhere now,' Hovendon said wearily. He studied Della. 'You figure she knows where he hid it?'

'If she does, I'll get it out of her once I got her in my jail.'

'What about the other one—Reneger?'

'He'll talk too, if need be.' The Marshal

109

hesitated, glanced at the two deputies moving up. 'Nothing, eh? Ain't surprised. Likely cached it somewheres close to town. Now, Sid, I want you and Mason to take your horses, get back in the brush and hide. When Reneger shows up, grab him, bring him in—best way you can.'

'We want him alive,' the cattleman said. 'Man dead can't do no talking.'

'Don't worry none about that,' the lawman said. 'Just bring him in ... I figure I'll find out all I want to know from her,' he added, ducking his head at Della.

CHAPTER FOURTEEN

Dan Reneger halted behind a low butte a quarter mile from the camp. When he did not meet Luke on the trail, the uneasiness within him built swiftly, and now, finally at the point where he could look into the clearing, that worry burst into full-fledged alarm.

The place was a shambles, appeared to have undergone a raid of some sort. There was no one in sight. Della and Luke's horses were missing—only the mules being in the rope corral.

He remained in the shadow of the rocky upthrust for a quarter hour, studying the meadow, trying to piece together any visible facts that would indicate what had taken place. The camp appeared deserted and the urge to ride in, have a closer inspection, was upon him, but deep in his mind, a small voice warned of imminent danger.

Again he thought of Apaches. A party of braves could have struck, moving in silently upon the Shofners, taking them unawares. Such would account for the solitary gunshot; but wouldn't raiding Indians have stripped the camp, and above all, taken the mules so highly prized by them?

Ordinarily, such could be expected, but he knew it was nothing to bank on. Circumstances altered situations, and a man could never be dead sure what an Apache would do. Outlaws? He had given that no thought. It could be ... It would account for Della's absence, but they would not have kidnapped Luke, too. Kill him, leave him lying in camp, yes.

The only answer was a closer look. He'd have to risk it. Raising himself in the stirrups, Dan followed out a line of brush with his eyes that would lead him, unseen, to a point below the clearing.

Wheeling the bay, he backtracked a short distance to the far side of the rank growth, and keeping near to it, rode down a sandy wash, eventually coming to the position he desired. He was below a slight embankment, could see nothing. Dismounting, he pulled the rifle from its scabbard, worked his way to the edge of the brush.

The camp was worse than it had appeared from the butte. Everything had been wrecked, torn apart—even the fire bin he had so recently built had been overturned, the stones scattered. He swore harshly, not understanding such malicious thoroughness. It was as if there had been a search for something.

His jaw tightened. A man had stepped from the piñons to the rear of the Shofner tent. An unfamiliar figure, he crossed to the front of the canvas shelter, picked something from the ground, hastily retraced his steps into the shadows. Straining to see better, Dan made out the shapes of two horses standing in a cleared space beyond the stranger.

They were waiting for him . . . An ambush . . .

He realized that instantly, realized also that there had been others in the party who had taken Della and Luke and gone on. Gone where?

Tracks . . . Several riders would leave hoof prints. They could not have gone west, or he would have encountered them; it was not possible, because of impassable cliffs, to go north—and to the south lay open country. Riders would be easily visible. It left only the

112

trail over the mountain that led to Frisco Springs. He'd look for tracks there.

Cautiously pulling himself half upright, he glanced around, got his bearings. The trail was to his right and a short distance in the direction of camp. He would be seen if he moved out from there, but by dropping back, cutting in until he was close to the foot of the slope, he could work forward unseen.

Immediately, he hurried back to the bay, and mounting, swung wide until he was hard against the base of the steep mountain side, and then headed for the trail. He reached it with no difficulty.

Dropping from the saddle, he began to prowl the lightly beaten path. He found the prints made earlier by his own party when they first rode in. And then, a bit to the left he discovered where four riders had come off the mountain, angled into camp. Five minutes later, he located another set of tracks made by four horses leaving the camp.

Squatting in the hot sunlight, he considered that. Four riders had come—later four had departed, heading up the trail for the settlement. At least two men had remained to ambush him . . . The answer was simple; two of the visitors had taken Della and Luke with them, heading, evidently, for Frisco Springs. The others were left to wait for him. Frowning, he tried to puzzle out a reason for all of it.

Suddenly, an angry core of suspicion began to build with Dan Reneger. Trask—goddam him—he had something to do with it! Earlier, he'd questioned Luke about the stage robbery; now, on the basis of some crazy, trumped-up charge, he'd come after him. Trask would do something like that; failing to find the real outlaw, he'd try hanging it on someone else to save his own face!

Burning, Reneger went to the saddle and started up the trail. He'd get to town quick, find Trask, and set him straight. Lawman or not, he had no right throwing his weight around just because he was having no luck finding the guilty man ... If, indeed, it had been Emil Trask ...

That thought came to Dan a short time later as he urged the bay along the path. It could be someone else—outlaws, as he had considered before. But that reasoning wouldn't hold up; they'd not head for town with their victims, nor would there have been two awaiting his return. It could only be the lawman.

He reached the outskirts of Frisco Springs just at dark, halted in the deep shade of a cottonwood at the end of the street. Light glowed in the windows of the Nugget, but Jess Pogue's establishment appeared to be about the only one to have turned up its lamps. He had only a dim view of the street from where he had stopped, and glancing about to be certain he was alone, he kneed the bay farther into the open. There was a light in Trask's office. Horses stood at the hitchrack.

If the Marshal were behind it, he'd be expected. Dan recognized that fact, crossed to the rear of the west row of business houses, and began a quiet approach to the jail through a welter of sheds, privies, and piles of trash.

Coming to the squat, barred window structure, he drew to a halt. Dismounting quietly, he tied the bay to a fence post, and drawing his rifle from the boot, stepped in close to the north wall of the building.

There was no window on that side. Moving silently, he worked his way through the shadows to the front, pulled up at the corner. One of the three horses at the rack was Della's black. Glowing with sudden anger, he turned the corner, started for the door. Emil Trask's harsh voice, coming from the interior, stopped him.

'You goddam little bitch—you ain't fooling me none! I know better'n that!'

Della's answer was defiant. 'He didn't tell me! You can keep on till doomsday, but it won't change that!'

A third voice, low and protesting, made a comment. Trask's reply was violent.

'Keep out of this—I know what I'm doing!

He admitted it, didn't he—or same as when I showed him that slicker and he went for his gun. Means he got the money, then hid it. Common sense'll tell you she was along when he hid it.'

Flat against the wall, Dan Reneger waited, listened. It sounded as if Luke were dead, that Trask was convinced he'd robbed the stagecoach and was now trying to force Della into telling where the money was hidden. He frowned. The Marshal would hardly go that far, unless—

'I'm waiting!'

Luke the outlaw—the holdup man? It was hard to believe. He would have recognized him—or would he? The low pulled hat, the cloth masking the face entirely, the full-length slicker ... Maybe—but it was hard to accept.

But, if true, it explained many things; Luke's sudden desire to break off the partnership, his urgent need to leave, his grand plans, the mystifying disinterest in horse ranching—something he'd professed to always hope for ... Maybe there was something to it, but as for Della, she'd be telling the truth. He'd swear to that.

'Last time I'm asking!' Emil Trask's tone was low, threatening. 'Where's that money hid?'

'I don't know.'

The sound of a sharp slap ended Della's

words, jolted a cry of pain from her lips. A gust of anger rocked Dan Reneger. All thoughts of personal involvement and its inevitable consequence dissolved in his mind. In three long strides, he crossed the front of the building. Rifle raised, he lunged through the doorway.

CHAPTER FIFTEEN

'Trask!'

At Reneger's sharp challenge, the lawman spun, hand dropping for the pistol at his side. Dan swung the rifle butt sideways, caught the lawman a blow on the head, sent him staggering against the wall. He recovered his balance, came up fast, then relaxed as he saw the muzzle of the rifle leveled at him.

Dan glanced to Della. She was on a chair near the cell. Her hair had come down, was hanging loosely about her shoulders; her face was swollen, discoloring where the Marshal's blows had fallen. But there was no submission in her.

She looked up at him, relief filling her eyes. And then that changed quickly to concern. 'You shouldn't have come. It'll mean—'

'Forget it!' he rasped, still torn by fury. He

117

motioned to Hovendon, crowded against the wall behind Trask's desk. 'Get your hands up—both of you! Turn around!'

The two men raised their arms higher. Reneger moved in quickly, lifted their pistols, threw them into a far corner.

'Shofner—where is he?'

Neither man answered. Dan repeated the question. Della roused. 'He's dead,' she replied woodenly. 'They—the Marshal shot him.'

Unreasoning fury gripped Reneger. Reaching out, he seized Trask's shoulder, spun him around.

'Why? damn you!'

Trask met his searing gaze unflinchingly. 'Resisted arrest, that's why.'

'For what? Another one of your cock and bull yarns?'

The lawman shook his head. 'Held up the stage, killed Oldaker. Know it for a fact. You still claim you didn't have a hand in it?'

'You know damned well I didn't—and I don't think Luke did either.'

Trask's features were stolid, but hatred burned in his eyes. 'Found his slicker. Had his name in it. Found the other stuff, too. Hovendon identified it. Was buried at the edge of town.'

The words heard outside the building were now making sense to Dan. 'He admit it?'

'Same as. Went for his gun when I jumped him about it.'

'No proof. Could have been some other reason. You rub a man wrong, Trask, make him want to fight.'

'He thinks I know where Luke hid the money,' Della said, brushing at her eyes. 'I don't ... He never said anything to me about a holdup.'

'She's lying,' Trask snapped. 'She was in on it right from the start—'

'If she says she wasn't, believe it,' Reneger cut in. He looked more closely at the girl, at her bruised features. A fresh wave of anger shook him. He took a half step toward Trask. 'Ought to cave your skull in, treating her like you have! Takes a brave man to work a woman over.'

Trask's agate eyes did not waver. 'Got a job to do, Mister, that's all. Do it the best way I know how—and you'd be smart to back off, keep your nose out of this. All I've got to do is send word to the U.S. Marshal in El Paso, and you're damn quick on the way to the pen.'

Reneger's voice was cold. 'I'd expect that of you, Marshal.'

Della rose, moved to his side, holding a small square of cloth to her cheek where blood had been brought to the surface.

'Like I said,' the lawman muttered, 'I do a job. Maybe I'll forget this clout to the head you just give me—but you'll have to take my advice, pull out.'

Hovendon nodded. 'Be the smart thing to do, Reneger.'

'Shofner and his woman were playing you for a sucker. Pretty sure of that now. Using you as a blind so's they could lay back, let things blow over.'

Dan felt Della's fingers on his arm. 'If you believe that, do it!' she said firmly. 'I can straighten this out.'

Reneger laughed, a short, harsh sound. 'With him?' he asked, ducking his head at the lawman. 'You think you'll ever make him believe you? He'd kill you trying to make you admit it. I know his kind. They're never wrong, and they bury their mistakes so nobody'll ever know the truth.'

'I'll get help,' she said stubbornly.

'Not around here. This is his town. Where's Luke's body?'

'Down the street ... The undertaker's, I guess.'

'He'll get looked after then. Can you ride?'

She stared up at him. 'What are you going to do?'

'Get out of here. Got to do it quick before somebody happens along.' He was thinking of the two men left at camp by Trask. When he failed to return, they'd eventually give up, report back to the lawman. And there was the very real possibility of some passerby

120

dropping in.

'Don't be a fool!' Trask warned, his voice rising. 'I'll put every lawman in the country on your trail.'

'Not for awhile, you won't' Dan said with a bleak smile. 'Get inside that cell—both of you.'

Hovendon turned obediently, stepped into the small cage. Trask, scowling, did not move. Reneger, impatient, stepped forward, pushed the lawman roughly, sent him stumbling in after the rancher. Slamming the door, he locked it. Keeping the ring of keys, he spun to Della.

'Come on.'

'Where can we go—hide?'

'Away from here for sure,' he said curtly, and taking her arm, started for the door.

'Reneger!' Trask shouted. 'You do this and—'

Dan, pushing the girl ahead of him, stepped into the open, pulled the panel shut. Finding the proper key, he locked it also. Then, glancing around, he tossed the ring onto the roof of the building on the opposite side of the street.

'That'll buy us a little time,' he said.

Helping Della to mount, he led her back to the rear of the building where the bay was tethered. Inside, they could hear Trask and Hovendon shouting, rattling the cell door. The sound was muted.

'Where can we go?' Della asked again as he swung onto the saddle and moved up beside her. He pointed to the alleyway, and they moved off.

'Only chance is to get out of the country,' he said. 'Be risky traveling the main roads. Best bet will be to double back to camp, pick up some grub, and head over the mountains for Colorado.'

She looked down, shook her head. 'I don't want to drag you into my trouble. If they catch you, it will mean—'

'Don't worry about it,' he said. 'First, they'll have to do that—catch me. Something was bound to happen, put me in bad, anyway.'

They reached the edge of the settlement. Dan cut off the road, chose a path running parallel but at a safe distance. 'Got to watch for that pair of deputies Trask left at camp. Expect they'll be along soon.'

He was feeling strangely lighthearted, as if he'd been released from some confining bond. The sense of being restricted, tied-down, forced to move and speak with caution was gone; and it was good. He had no regrets. As he had told Della, he had known, deep within him, that eventually trouble would overtake him. Well, they'd have a hard time tracking him—he'd make damned sure of that.

But what of Della?

He glanced at her, wondered if that had been the true purpose and meaning of her repeated question. Was she worried about her own future?

'Can put you on a stage once we're clear of the territory, head you back to your home in Kansas,' he said.

She looked at him, faintly surprised, not expecting an answer after so long a time. She moved her head in agreement, stared off into the starlit night.

'Be safe. Trask'll never think to look for you there. Nobody around Frisco Springs knows where you hail from, do they?'

'No—unless Luke mentioned it.'

That wasn't likely, Dan decided. He continued to study her, noted the drawn lines of her face. 'What happened to Luke—was a bad thing for you to see.'

Her shoulders stirred. 'It was all over with so quick—and I kept praying for you to come.' Her words broke off abruptly. 'I guess we were both wrong about him.'

Reneger started to reply, lifted his hand warningly. Off to the right, the rapid drumming of horses was a steady sound in the cool night.

'Trask's deputies,' he said. 'Means we won't have much time. They'll head for the jail.' He looked at her. 'Can you make it?'

Della was numb with weariness. Her entire body seemed to sag, and her hair, still loose, fluttered in the light breeze.

'I'll keep up,' she said.

At once, he spurred the bay into a lope, angling now for the road, finally safe, where it would be easier traveling and faster time could be made.

They crossed the mountain without rest, came down into the ghostly, deserted camp about midnight. Immediately, Dan dismounted, hurried to Della's side. Lifting her exhausted body from the saddle, he carried her to where several blankets had been tossed and placed her upon them.

'Stay put while I get some grub together.'

She struggled to rise. 'I can help—'

'Be quicker if I do it,' he said, and pressing her back, turned away.

Snatching up an empty flour sack, he stuffed it with coffee, dried meats, potatoes, biscuits, and several other articles of food he found readily available. They'd not take one of the mules; a pack animal would slow them too much.

Enough food to last, he rolled blankets into separate cylinders, lashed them securely to their saddles, and then taking the canteens, filled them at the creek. Likely they would cross streams on the journey north, but he would take no chances. That chore done, he halted in the center of the camp, glanced about, searching for anything else they might have need of.

His gun...

He hastened to where his bedroll lay. It had been pulled apart by Trask's men. Anxious, he dug into it, probed around until he found the coiled belt with its holster and worn-handled pistol. Relieved, he pulled it free, strapped it on. Drawing the heavy weapon, he spun the cylinder to check its loads, then returned it to its oiled leather casing. The weight of it felt good against his leg.

Wheeling, he trotted to the rope corral, freed the mules so that they might forage for themselves, and then retraced his step to where Della lay. Her eyes were closed, and he thought she was sleeping, but at his approach she sat up.

'Ready,' he said, extending his hand. 'We get back in the hills a piece, you can rest again.'

She rose slowly, her gaze on the pistol hanging at his side. She started to make some comment, shrugged, and turned toward her horse.

'I'll be all right,' she murmured. 'I just want to get away from here.'

CHAPTER SIXTEEN

Emil Trask watched the outer door to his office close, heard the lock click. He stepped back from the bars of the cell, body trembling violently, eyes flaming as an ungovernable rage swept through him.

'Goddam that Reneger to hell! I'll kill him, by God—I'll track him down ... Him and that woman ... Time I'm through with them, they'll be begging to die!'

Cal Hovendon, jaw sagging, stared at the lawman as if transfixed. After a moment, he reached out, laid a cautious hand on the Marshal's heaving shoulder.

'It's all right, Emil,' he said hesitantly. 'Ain't no use getting so worked up ... Somebody'll be coming along—'

'Hell with you!' Trask shouted, knocking the rancher's arm away. 'If I hadn't listened to you—'

'Me? What did I say?'

'Too damned much ... Whining and complaining all the time ...'

Trask's words trailed off into a rumble of cursing. Grasping the bars of the cell door with both hands, he rattled the grill vigorously.

'Somebody out there in the street—come in here! Help!'

There was no answering hail. Sweating heavily, the lawman brushed nervously at his strained face. Cal Hovendon had drawn away from him and seated himself on the end of the cot in the opposite corner.

'Settle down, Emil,' he said, his tone quiet, guarded. He knew the Marshal for a hard, rough man who leaned to violence. He had seen him in action several times around town, and just that night when he was attempting to make the Shofner woman talk, but he had not realized Trask could lose control of himself so completely. It was almost a madness.

'Have to wait for daylight to start tracking them, anyway.'

'Daylight!' Trask shouted. 'That bastard and the woman'll be thirty miles from here by then!'

'Can head them off—send word to all the towns around.'

'Hell with that! I want them myself ... Ain't nobody else getting them ... They're paying me—paying me plenty for what they've done.'

'Kill that girl, and I'll never get my money back.'

The lawman spun. His eyes still glowed, and his hands clenched and opened spasmodically. 'You know something, Mister Big Rancher? I don't give a goddam whether you do or not! What do you think of that?'

Hovendon's face blanched, and then an angry flush began to mount his cheeks. 'What do I think? I'm thinking maybe we've got the wrong man wearing the Marshal's badge in this town.'

Emil Trask stared, taken aback by the cattleman's unexpected display of boldness, but as fury again rushed through him, he took a threatening step toward the rancher. Hovendon drew back.

'You do, eh? Well, you got me to thank there ain't more like Shofner and Reneger hanging around this country ... Ain't that right?'

Hovendon nodded slowly. 'Reckon so.'

'You reckon? You know goddam well it's the truth!'

Wheeling, the lawman began to rattle the cell door once more, shouting as he did. When again there was no response, he withdrew to a corner of the cage, leaned dejectedly against the bars.

'Damn him ... Damn him ... Damn him,' he muttered over and over in a bitter tone. 'Locking me in my own jail—hitting me with that rifle ... I'll—'

Anger was draining from him. The heaving of his chest lessened, and he was becoming quieter. After a few minutes he crossed the cell, sat down on the end of the cot opposite Cal Hovendon. Leaning forward, elbows on knees, he buried his face in his hands.

There was absolute silence within the jail. No sound from the outside, not even the tumultuous racket from the Nugget penetrated the thick, adobe walls, and with the doors closed, the stale, heated air was suffocating.

Hovendon, worn from the continual search for the holdup man, dozed fitfully, back resting against the wall of the cell. Several times, he roused, glanced to the lawman. Trask never moved. The rancher had small hopes of someone dropping by. Emil Trask had no friends. There'd be no one, seeing the light, stopping in to talk, pass the time. They'd simply have to wait until daylight when the attention of some passerby could be attracted.

Abruptly, he straightened as the sound of horses in front of the building came to him. Trask heard it also, sprang to his feet, crossed to the front of the cell.

'That's them!' he shouted.

Hovendon got to his feet. 'Who?'

'Mason and Sid ... It'd better be them—if they're dumb enough to still be waiting there at that camp for Reneger, I'll skin them alive!'

The outer door rattled. A voice called out: 'You in there, Marshal?'

'Hell, yes, I'm in here! Door's locked. Break it down!'

There was a long pause. Then Mason asked: 'What'd you say?' There was a note of doubt in his voice.

'Kick that door in, goddammit! I'm locked in.'

The lower panel splintered as it gave way under the drive of the deputy's boot. The knob twisted, but the lock continued to hold. At the next onslaught the entire door flew open, crashed against the wall. The deputies stumbled in, came to a halt in the center of the room.

'You locked in the cell, too?' Sid asked, staring.

'What's it look like?' Trask demanded. 'Get the keys. Laying outside somewheres, Likely near the stoop.'

Both deputies wheeled, hastily moved through the doorway, and began to search the area fronting the building. Fuming, Trask let it run on for several minutes.

'Forget it!' he yelled finally. 'Bastard probably took the ring with him. Get a crowbar. Have to pry the lock open.'

Mason took off at a fast trot for the blacksmith's shop. He was back in ten minutes, breathing heavily from his exertions.

'Jackson wasn't around ... Had to hunt a bit,' he explained apologetically.

'All right, all right,' the lawman said impatiently. 'Just get me out of here.'

Mason inserted the wedge end of the tool between the bars below the lock. Then, with Sid adding his weight, he threw his body against the crowbar. The door popped open with a clang.

Emil Trask, suddenly cool and deadly serious, stepped forward quickly. 'Let's get after them,' he said.

'After who?' Mason wondered. 'You ain't told us nothing—'

'Reneger and that woman. Tricked me, got away two, three hours ago.'

'That's how come he never showed up at the camp!' Sid exclaimed. 'Was here all the time.'

Trask ignored the deputy. 'Want a posse. Half a dozen or so men. Get Joe Rapp. Be needing him for tracking.'

Mason wagged his head. 'This time of night, Marshal, ain't sure I can get anybody.'

'And we ain't had no sleep or nothing to eat,' Sid added. 'I'm plumb beat.'

'Get yourself a bite at Pogue's while you're rounding up the posse. Can sleep in the saddle.'

Sid groaned. 'Doubt if I can even set upon a horse ... Can't we hold off till daylight?'

'No, we can't!' Trask replied curtly. 'They've got a hell of a long start on us now.'

Mason and Sid, both grumbling, started for the door. Hovendon, conscious of the chameleonlike change in Emil Trask's

131

manner—from a violent, near maniacal man to one now quiet, efficient, dedicated to the job at hand—crossed to the corner of the office, retrieved his pistol and that of the lawman.

'Which way you figure they went?' he asked, passing the Marshal's weapon to him.

Trask inspected his pistol, shoved it into its holster. 'Rapp'll figure that out. Back to the Buttes, I'd guess. Be needing supplies for the trail. Only place they can get them.'

'Where'd they go from there?' Hovendon said protestingly. 'Hard to get out of that country—nothing but box canyons, palisades.'

Trask grinned smugly. 'We know that,' he said. 'Reneger don't.'

★　　★　　★

A short distance beyond the canyon where he had intended to erect the first mustang trap, Dan Reneger pulled to a halt. Della could go no farther. Worn to exhaustion from the ride to town and back, shattered by the experiences she had been through, it was all she could do to stay on her horse.

Dismounting, he pulled the blanket from his saddle, folded it lengthwise, and laid a pallet beneath the overhang of a projecting rock. He turned then, lifting her from the black.

132

Her eyes flew open, and she began to fight him, struggling violently.

'It's all right,' he said, calming her.

When she was quiet, he carried her to the bed he'd made and laid her upon it. Taking the second blanket, he covered her.

She watched him with dull interest. 'Will it be safe to stop?'

'For a while,' he said. 'I'll wake you when it's time to move on.'

She was asleep almost instantly, a slight frown on her face. Reneger stood for a brief minute looking down at her, and turned away.

They'd not be able to halt for long. Emil Trask would quickly organize his posse and be on their trail; perhaps it was under way at that very moment. He'd need to watch sharp ... One fact was definite in his mind; the lawman would never again get Della in his hands.

CHAPTER SEVENTEEN

Reneger awoke with a start. Cursing, he leaped to his feet, alarm rushing through him as he glanced to the east. Faint pearl was lighting the horizon, and dawn was not far off. How long had he slept? He had intended to rest only for a few minutes; he apparently had lost two or three hours.

He looked at Della. She lay motionless on her pallet beneath the ledge. Turned to him, her features, despite the slight swellings, were soft-edged, serene. He felt something within him stir, and the deep loneliness with which he'd lived for so many years set up its voiceless clamor.

But as in times past, he ignored it; such was not for him. Always, there was overruling reason—a cold practicality that denied him a way of life so readily accepted and taken for granted by other men. He had nothing to offer any woman—no future, no security, not even the means for providing the barest of necessities. It might have come to pass had his plans for a horse ranch materialized, but that, too, was a failure.

And Man once more was his enemy. He was outside the law, not by choice at the onset but by accident; now, it was by willful decision, since he had elected to stand by a friend and the woman who was his wife. He shrugged wearily. It was always the unexpected things that trip a man, wreck his hopes.

Still disturbed and impatient with his thoughts, he walked quietly from the coulee where they had halted to a bald knob a short distance away. From there, he could look back over the broken land, see to the slope near which the camp had been built.

Tension within him eased. He could detect no movement and guessed there had not been time enough for Trask and the men making up a posse to get on their trail. But he could not be sure. It was still too dark to see clearly. Beyond a short range, everything was a confusion of shadows; the brush assumed odd shapes; the rocks, even the squat trees, were grotesque, unfamiliar.

But he felt they were safe for at least a while. He doubted if the Marshal and Cal Hovendon had been released before the two deputies had arrived at the jail. Then would have followed the time-consuming chore of opening the cell when no keys were available. After that would come the arranging for a posse and the decision as to which direction the fugitives had taken.

Trask would expect them to go north, the only logical route—but he would not be sure. He'd take no chances, call in a tracker, and picking up the hoof prints at the rear of the jail, start from there. Darkness would hinder the operation to some extent—he might even delay until sunrise—but eventually, the lawman would come.

And the chase would be on. Reneger stared into the distance. If he didn't have Della with him, he'd swing west, make a run for it through the barren country of the Apaches beyond the hills. He couldn't risk it with her. There was only one way open—work higher into the mountains, try to reach the far side, and hope that safety and escape could be found there.

They might as well have a morning meal. He came off the knob, retraced his steps to the coulee. Della still slept, lips fluttering with her regular breathing. Moving quietly, he obtained the small lard bucket he carried in his saddlebags and filled it half full of water from one of the canteens.

Taking it to the opposite side of the shallow basin, he selected a spot behind another sandstone upthrust where glare would not be noticed and built a small fire. Balancing the tin on several flat stones hastily pulled together about the flames, he removed a quantity of bacon, a can of beans, and some biscuits from the sack of provisions. All these he dumped into a cast-iron skillet which he also placed on the fire.

That done, he saw to the horses, treating them to a small amount of water poured into his hat. The drink would have to last them the entire day, unless they were fortunate enough to encounter a spring or stream.

He stood then looking off toward the summit of the mountains rising steeply before him. It was forbidding country in the early light. A world of ragged peaks piercing the gray sky; of long ridges dark with pines and scrub oak; of sheer palisades, rocky

136

slides, canyons, and deep saddles. He hoped they could make it through—and then, thinking of Emil Trask, he knew they must.

He moved the horses to a different spot, where they could enjoy better grazing, and returned to the fire. The bacon was beginning to sizzle and set up its inviting aroma, but the water in the bucket was barely warm. He added more fuel to the flames and paused, hearing Della's step. She knelt beside him.

'Here, let me do that,' she said, taking up a stick and stirring the contents of the spider. 'Don't we have a spoon?'

He grinned at her, struck by the commonplace of the observation, crossed to where he had hung the supply sack, and dug out plates, cups, and the necessary hand tools. There was no nonsense to Della Shofner; she knew what had to be done, how to do it, and went about accomplishing the fact calmly.

Handing her the spoon, he placed the rest of the items on a nearby rock and reached for the sack of coffee. Taking a generous handful, he dumped it into the lard tin.

'Why did you let me sleep so long?' Della asked without looking up. Her voice contained a disapproving note.

'You needed rest. Was only a couple of hours.'

She glanced to the steadily brightening

137

east. 'Aren't we taking a risk?'

'Maybe ... Still got a good lead.'

She continued to stir the mixture in the skillet. The coffee boiled up suddenly. Reneger set it off the fire, whipped down the brown froth with a twig, returned it to the edge of the flames.

Della glanced to the towering, rugged facade to the north. She shuddered. 'The mountains look so high, so—so unfriendly. Isn't there some other way we can go?'

He shook his head. 'The only one.'

She removed the spider, rose, and taking the plates, filled each. The beans, flavored by the bacon, were savory, and the heat and moisture had softened the biscuits. Pouring their cups full of coffee, Reneger settled back, sighing deeply.

'Going to taste good. Seems like weeks since I had a meal.'

She toyed with the food. 'Everything seems long ago.'

She was thinking of Luke, he knew, and so said nothing. Whatever her thoughts, they were hers alone, and he had no wish to intrude. If she desired, she would speak of them.

'It's hard to believe Luke's gone—dead,' she murmured.

Reneger sipped at his coffee. 'Things happen fast,' he said, at a loss for words.

She leaned forward, face intent. 'I want

you to know the truth, Dan. I didn't know about the robbery, and I don't know anything about all that money or where he hid it.'

'You didn't have to tell me that.'

'And another thing—we weren't using you, like the Marshal claimed ... At least, I wasn't.'

'No need to say that either.'

'But it's important to me that you're sure. It surprised me as much as it did you—even Luke's wanting to break up the partnership and go away. First I heard of that was when he told you.'

'Can see now why he changed his mind. He figured on that money—the twenty thousand he'd taken from Cal Hovendon—to do all those things he planned. Guess the Marshal was partly right. Luke did make use of the partnership that much.'

'I think he really intended to go through with it at the start. He must have heard about the money after we got to Frisco Springs and decided to hold up that stage. How he found out about all that cash—'

'Not hard to figure,' Reneger said, shrugging. 'Hovendon's got a loud mouth. Expect half the territory knew. Surprised somebody else didn't get to him before Luke did.'

Dan set his empty plate to one side and

helped himself to more coffee. He looked at Della keenly.

'Miss him?'

She stared into the fire. After a moment, she faced him squarely. 'Maybe it's wrong to feel the way I do,' she said, honestly, 'but—no, I don't. Not really.'

'But I thought—'

'What Luke told you about us wasn't exactly true. Oh, we grew up on farms that are next to each other, and I guess I liked him when I was small—young. But he went away, and I got over it.'

'You married him.'

She stirred. 'I know—and I'm not sure why. I think maybe it was the excitement of it, or the chance to get away from the farm ... I hardly knew Luke.'

'Yet—'

'Yet, I married him,' she broke in. 'Yes, I know. Don't ask me to explain why. I've asked myself the same question a dozen times, and the only answer I could find is what I've told you ... But it's finished now—and you've been dragged into it. I'm sorry, Dan.'

'Don't be.'

'All your fine plans. It's too bad—you'd have done well.'

'Maybe. Man never knows how things'll turn out.'

'Where'll you go, once we're out of the

territory, I mean?'

'Montana ... Wyoming ... Hard to say. Found out a long time ago that there's little sense in looking too far ahead. Always something comes along, changes your thinking. Best way is to take it a day at a time.'

There was bitterness in his voice, as if too many things had gone wrong in the past for him and he had come finally to accept the inevitable.

'You'll get another chance,' Della said. 'I'm sure of it.'

'Not looking for one,' he replied. 'Don't intend to make it easy for some tin badge. I'll keep moving, not stay long in any one place.'

Della's lips tightened with anger. 'Can't something be done about—about this probation thing? Why can't you go to the governor, or somebody high up like him, get it stopped? Luke said it wasn't right, that the judge was unfair, took his spite out on you.'

'Still a judge, and his word stands. Anyway, what would I tell the governor— that the law was picking on me?'

She looked away. 'No, I guess not.'

Dan Reneger was not one to beg favors, she knew. He'd been handed a raw deal, and he'd live with it, not complain. She watched him get to his feet, tall, angular, his eyes deep-pocketed and colorless in the rising light. A dark stubble covered his cheeks and chin, lent him a stern, unrelenting image.

Silent, he began to collect the dishes and utensils they had used. She rose, gave him her help. When that was done, he crossed to the horses and began to tighten the cinches, prepare them for the day.

A broad blaze of yellow was now flaring the east, and long fingers of delicate orange and palest red were spearing the sky. Below them, the buttes and slopes were changing to lighter browns and greens, and the blackness of the piñons and cedars was fading to a more familiar shade.

When the horses were ready, he led them down into the coulee. Hanging the sack of provisions upon his saddle, he returned the rolled blankets to their place, and then facing Della, helped her mount. Climbing onto the bay, he angled across the swale to its lip for a final look at the lower trail. The muscles of his jaw tightened.

Four riders were moving across the flat.

CHAPTER EIGHTEEN

Reneger squinted into the glare. Only four men. Trask apparently had difficulty in raising a posse at such an hour of the night. Likely the same men accompanied him as before—Cal Hovendon and the two deputies.

That assumption changed a moment later. One of the riders moved to the front, dismounted. Kneeling, he examined the trail ... A tracker ... The Marshal was taking no chances on losing them. He swore softly, wished he'd taken time to cover their tracks. If he'd done so at the jail, they might yet be free of pursuit ... But there is never any profit in wishing.

Wheeling, he returned to Della. 'We've got company,' he said matter of factly.

Concern filled her eyes. 'The Marshal?'

'Him and three others. One's a tracker.'

'Are they close?'

Reneger shook his head. 'Pretty far yet.'

Spurring the bay, he rode out of the coulee onto the rocky path. Della swung in behind. The slope was brightening swiftly now. High up on the crags and ridges, sunlight was already visible and beginning to spread downward, wiping out the pockets of shadow, bringing the crevices into distinction and varying the colors of the escarpments.

But the early morning chill still held, as if the night were unwilling to give way to day, and when Dan glanced back, he saw Della had taken her blanket and wore it now about her shoulders as a shawl.

'Be warm—soon as the sun hits us,' he called.

She smiled. 'I'll be fine.'

A vicious country, he thought, turning his attention again to the trail. Freeze at night, roast during the day—never any happy in-between. But he knew he would have it no other way. The country was in his blood, the vast land was a part of him, even as he was a part of it—and from it, he'd never be driven, even though lawmen prowled his footsteps and a threat forever would hang, like a Damoclean sword, over his head.

They climbed steadily. Several times, Dan looked back, seeking the whereabouts of the posse, but the edge of the slope up which they traveled broke sharply, and all below was hidden from view. They were there, however—four dogged, patient hunters; he knew that without doubt. It was the measure of distance that separated them from him that was of interest.

An hour later, he had his first glimpse of the party. The riders were disturbingly close, and that gave rise to brief worry, until he realized they would have made fast time crossing the fairly level flat while he and Della were compelled to toil upward slowly.

Their progress would now show a marked decrease, and likely they could do no more than keep pace. He could distinguish the men: Hovendon; one of the deputies he had seen at the camp; the tracker, a small, thin-bodied man with a yellow beard; and, of

144

course, Emil Trask.

He should do something about the tracks they were leaving, he decided. The thought came a little late, but if he could confuse the posse for only a few minutes, it would help. Time might come when every second would count. Looking ahead, he saw only the narrow defile through which the trail carved its steep course. No opportunity there, but on beyond a shoulder of rock, the path appeared to fall away, slide down into a small wash.

Urging the bay to a trot, he gained the false crest, grunted in satisfaction. Several side canyons turned off, draining into what was a shallow basin. The trail bisected the swale exactly, resuming its grade on the yonder side. Perhaps here he could create delay, throw off Trask and the others for a few precious minutes.

He turned to Della, pointed to the largest of the arroyos. 'Head in there.'

She moved out immediately without question. He veered in behind her, holding the bay slightly to one side in order for two sets of hoof prints to be clearly visible.

They continued up the slash for several yards, fighting the dense brush, until the slopes began to close in, and then, on a gravelly bench, wheeled around. Staying in the underbrush, and now in front of Della, Reneger slanted across the rough rise and

145

rejoined the trail some distance above the point where they had swung off. He halted there, handed the reins of the bay to the girl.

'Keep going. I'll catch up.'

As before, she voiced no question, simply resumed the climb. Dan, ripping a branch from a clump of mountain mahogany, followed, brushing out all signs of their passage with the length of brush. He kept at it for a long hundred yards, finally tossed the branch over the edge of the cliff, and mounted the bay.

'Ought to slow them down a bit,' he said, wiping at the sweat on his brow. Heat was beginning to make itself a factor, and both horses were working into a lather. They'd need rest soon. The grade was steep.

'Still a long way to the top,' Della said, lifting her eyes to the gray-green rim far above. 'Seems like we get no closer.'

'Covered about a third of the way, I'd judge,' Dan replied. He fell silent, watched her turn and look down the trail. It was still empty.

'We'll make it,' he said confidently.

He wished he felt as certain now as he had at the beginning, but in his mind, a different sort of worry was making itself known. The canyon seemed to be growing narrower. Rock slides were more numerous, and through the thinning trees, he could see sheer walls of granite rising to various levels, all well above them.

He said nothing to Della, however, as tension continued to build within him, and they pressed on through the close heat trapped within the walls.

The trail began to curve ... Dan felt a stir of relief. Evidently, the path doubled back, whipped its way in a series of horseshoe bends to gain the ledges above. They completed the curve and paused on its outermost edge to breathe the horses and look into the canyon.

The trail fell away below them in an almost straight line. He saw the rise where the shoulder of rock marked the entrance into the basin, located the arroyo into which he and Della had turned in hopes of confusing Trask and making him think they were attempting to cut directly across the mountain.

In that next moment, he watched the lawman and his party round the shoulder and continue on, ignoring the lapse in the tracks.

Realization struck him with solid force. No longer were they being trailed; there was no need. They were in a dead-end canyon. This Emil Trask knew.

'Dan—what's wrong?'

Della's voice jarred him. He faced her soberly. There was no sense in keeping it from her. 'They've got us trapped. We're in a box canyon.'

There was no panic in her eyes, no soaring fear, only a quiet concern. 'What can we do?'

I can shoot it out with the bastards, give the law an honest reason for hunting me down, he thought, but he had Della to consider.

An idea came to him. Trask and his men had ignored the ruse at the arroyo. They might do it again if he stayed in sight, used himself as bait. Rising in the stirrups, he scanned the trail. There were several washes to the inside, all small but filled with rock and brush.

'Come on,' he said tersely, and spurred the bay into sudden motion.

They swept around the bend and once more began the climb against the face of the cliff. A deep shadowed arroyo appeared almost immediately. Reneger halted, pointed.

'In there,' he said. 'Hurry!'

CHAPTER NINETEEN

For the first time, Della showed a reluctance to follow his direction. She frowned. 'Aren't you—'

'No,' he cut her short. 'Pull in there—get back far as you can, and keep quiet. I'm going on up trail. Want them to spot me so's they'll come on by.'

'And then?'

Ignoring the question, he thrust his hand inside his shirt, unsnapped one of the pockets of his money belt. Obtaining several gold coins, he passed them to her.

'You'll need these ... Don't worry about me. I'll be close by.'

Suspicions fully aroused, she stared at the coins and then at him. 'What're these for? Why will I need them?'

'Fare—expenses, so you can get home,' he said impatiently.

'Home? I don't understand.'

'You're to hide in that arroyo,' he explained. 'They'll ride by, follow me. Once they've passed, you head back down the trail.'

Her chin set stubbornly. 'And leave you here to face them when it's my trouble, not yours?'

'Don't argue with me' he snapped. 'They're close.' Abruptly, his gruff manner changed. 'It'll work out. When they see you're not with me, chances are good I can straighten things out for myself.'

It was a lie. Nothing he could say or do now would ever pacify Emil Trask, he knew, but he had to overcome her unwillingness, make her see reason.

'I won't know where to go,' she said, finally accepting his instructions. 'This country is all strange.'

'No problem ... Head back the way we came. It'll take you by our camp. You know the trail from there to town?'

She nodded. 'Over the mountain.'

'Just follow it until you get to the flats on the other side. Turn north—that'll be your left. Frisco Springs will lay to your right. Better not go there.'

'Is there another town nearby?'

'About thirty miles—north. Make it there, and you can catch a stagecoach east.' He glanced down the canyon. 'You'll have to hurry.'

She put the black into motion, pointing him directly into the narrow, brushy mouth of the wash. The horse fought the bit for a moment, then lowering his head, shouldered in. Halfway, Della stopped him, looked at Dan.

'I don't feel right doing this—leaving you to face my trouble.'

He grinned. 'It'll work out. Do what I tell you. Let them go by. Give them a little time, then start back. Walk your horse for the first mile. Don't want them hearing him. Understand?'

She nodded and smiled forlornly. 'Guess this is good-bye, Dan. Will we ever meet again?'

'Who knows? Chances are I'll be up Kansas way someday.'

150

'I'll keep looking for you,' she said in a low voice.

'Do that,' he said, and moving forward, slapped the black smartly on the rump and sent him plunging ahead into the arroyo.

Losing no more time, Reneger dropped to the ground, brushed out the tracks entering the wash, and then swinging onto the bay, resumed the trail. It was a good spot. Trask and the others would be looking forward, seeking the end of the canyon, which could not be far distant now. Odds were they'd never notice the arroyo, much less suspect Della to be hiding in it.

He urged the gelding to a faster pace, turning a deaf ear to the animal's labored breathing. At every opportunity, he kept to the outer edge of the trail, hoping to make himself clearly visible to the men below. With luck, the end of the box would be a mile yet; he wanted the showdown to come as far from Della as possible.

Della ... He thought of her, realized he missed having her with him. She had proved to be everything he thought she was not—and he was regretting the sharp words he had spoken at their first meeting ... Maybe this would make up for it, let her know how he really felt.

A hell of a way for a girl's marriage to end—husband killed before her eyes; now high in a wild and strange country running for her life. She deserved none of it ... And she had deserved better than Luke Shofner, too, who had gotten her into such trouble. Goddam Luke, anyway, he was at the bottom of all of it. He'd sure been fooled by Shofner, had figured him for a better man.

Luke had fooled Della, too, he knew that now. And maybe Della had deceived herself a little about him. But it wasn't the first time a woman had grasped the opportunity to escape a humdrum life—and certainly, she wouldn't be the last. But he wished things could have turned out better for her. Perhaps now they would. Once back in Kansas, on safe, familiar ground, she could start a new life. She was still young enough.

The sudden crack of a rifle split the quiet, set up a chain of echoes through the canyon. Reneger spun, spurred the bay to the back side of the cliff. The bullet had struck above him, clipping viciously through the leaves of a scrub oak.

Jerking his rifle from its boot, he trotted to the edge of the trail, dropped to his belly, and peered over. Surprise rippled through him. He had no idea the posse was so near. They were still below the arroyo where Della was hiding, but they had gained amazingly.

It was the deputy who had fired the shot. The man was standing in his stirrups, neck craned, trying to line up a second try. Dan laid his rifle across a rock and sighted down the barrel. The riders were a good 250 yards below and to his right. It would be a difficult shot.

He pulled back, considered his position. It would be unwise to make a stand there. Trask and the posse must be led past the arroyo, brought to a point farther up the trail, so that Della would have her opportunity for escape. But to—

A bullet slapped into the rock upon which he had laid his rifle, sending up a puff of fine dust, peppering his face and neck with stinging particles of stone. A curse ripped from his lips. He'd lain there like a fool, leaving himself exposed.

Angered, he hunched over his rifle, lined the sights again. Allowing for distance and fall, he pressed off the trigger. The deputy flinched, rocked on his saddle.

Instantly, Reneger regretted his actions, not for the sake of the deputy but because he had circumvented the very thing he hoped to accomplish—draw the posse safely by Della's hiding place. Leaping to his feet, he hurried to the extreme lip of the trail, presented himself boldly. He remained there for a few moments, and then wheeling, trotted to his horse, mounted, and still in view, headed up the narrow path.

Rounding a short bend, he pulled in the bay. A sheer wall of ragged granite, rising 100 feet, loomed before him. This was the end of the canyon—the end of the trail.

Grim, he twisted about, stared down the slope. No one was in sight yet. Dropping from the saddle, he again drew his rifle, walked to the edge of the small, circular flat lying at the base of the cliff. It was a vertical drop to a ledge a full 100 feet below ... No escape on that side—or approach either. That had been the only possibility. All else was rock wall.

Leading the bay to a stunted juniper at the fringe of the clearing, he crossed to the base of the palisade, where boulders, dislodged from above, had fallen to form an unlevel, craggy mound. From there, he would have full vision of the trail's entrance, as well as a degree of protection.

Climbing into the welter of rocks, he settled down to wait.

CHAPTER TWENTY

Alone in the brush-filled arroyo, Della listened to the hollow thud of Reneger's horse as it moved up the trail. A tremor raced through her, and for a few moments, she knew fear such as she had never before experienced, and then she calmed. Dan had fixed it so that she would be safe, could go free. Everything would be all right.

A different feeling possessed her when she was with him. She felt strong, confident, unafraid. She took that from him, she guessed, in a sort of absorption. It hadn't been so with Luke. In the brief time they'd been together, he'd given her nothing, only taken, and in her mind, he was now the less for it.

But she was doomed to lose Dan Reneger, even as she had lost Luke.

She stood quiet in the brush, thinking of that. Dan had sought to make her believe he would be all right, that once she escaped, he would be able to settle with Emil Trask ... And she had believed him—at least, she had accepted his words as truth when he spoke them. Now that she was having time to think it over, she realized he had merely convinced her for her own sake.

Dan Reneger would die. He'd reach the end of the canyon, and then in that quiet, matter-of-fact way of his, make a stand. Trask and the others would come—and there would be a fight until he was dead.

He's doing it for me, she thought bitterly. It had been none of his affair. He'd come to the Butte country, bringing the money he'd scrimped and saved for years, probably, to fulfill a long-standing dream. A lonely man walking under a shadow, he'd wanted only to be left alone, pursue the sort of life he chose.

Instead, he'd been betrayed by a man he

thought was a friend, drawn into an ugly incident that, even though proven innocent of involvement, would result in imprisonment.

She had complicated it, made it worse for him. True, she hadn't asked him to step in, stand by her, but being the sort of man he was, he had done so unbidden, the solid manhood of him refusing to ignore her plight, demanding that he give her his strength and protection.

It would cost him his life. Her lips compressed as cool determination moved through her. She turned, glanced at the saddle of her horse. The rifle Luke had given her was in its scabbard ... She'd not let Dan Reneger face the posse alone. She'd let them pass by, and then, instead of fleeing for her life, she'd slip out, follow. When they discovered they had rifles pointed at them from two sides, they'd think twice before starting a shoot-out.

The black shifted nervously, uncomfortable in the crowding brush. Della listened, endeavoring to locate the oncoming riders. She could hear nothing and concluded they were still some distance down the trail.

Moving quietly, she devoted the next two or three minutes trying to enlarge the space around the black by pushing away the overhanging limbs and branches that annoyed him. For the horse to shift and shake himself at the wrong moment would prove disastrous.

Suddenly, the canyon echoed with a gunshot. Della jumped, startled by the report. It came from somewhere on the trail and a short distance below the arroyo. She waited, scarcely breathing as concern gripped her. Had Dan been hit? Had they taken him unawares, caught him silhouetted on the path above, put a bullet into him? Time dragged agonizingly. There was no answering shot from higher on the slope. Her fears mounted higher.

A second blast shattered the hush, again from below the arroyo. And then within only seconds, a rifle fired from above. A man yelled in pain. Della sighed with relief. Dan was still alive! His bullet had hit one of the posse members.

She smiled, picturing him somewhere high on the trail. He'd be like a wolf at bay, a fierce, dangerous wolf ready for a fight to the finish, regardless of the odds. Trask and his men would move with greater care now, and that would help her, make it easier for her to slip in, get behind them. They'd be so intent on Dan none would suspect her of taking a hand.

She heard the click of a hoof against stone. The black, hearing it also, jerked his head, set up a faint jingle of harness metal. The posse was near, proceeding slowly, cautiously. She glanced at the black, prayed he would remain quiet. A man's voice—the Marshal's, she thought—said something in a low, angry tone. There was an answer, but she—

The brush parted, and a man stood before her. A squat, ugly man with matted, tobacco-stained beard and dressed in filthy, ill-smelling deerskins. He grinned at her, exposing irregular, broken teeth. His eyes, small and sharp, looked her up and down.

'Ain't nobody ever fooled old Joe Rapp, lady,' he drawled. 'Not even the Injuns.' Twisting his shaggy head, he called: 'H'yeh's the gal, Marshal.'

Frozen, voiceless, Della heard the thud of boot heels hitting the trail, the rattle of brush. Emil Trask, followed closely by Hovendon, moved up beside Rapp.

The lawman glared at her. 'Trying to outfox me, eh?'

Fear locked Della in its tight grip, and then the greater strength of hate released her. She had a flooding recollection of the hours in Trask's jail, of his brutal treatment, of the shocking blows that had driven her to her knees. She whirled, sprang for the rifle on her saddle. Her fingers closed about the stock, dragged it clear.

Trask's knotted fist caught her a stunning blow on the head. Her senses reeled, and the rifle flew from her grasp. A second blow drove her to the ground. Trask seized her loosely spilling hair, and as he had done once before, jerked back her head, forced her to look up into his angry, sweat-covered face.

'Be none of that!' he snarled.

Della choked off a cry. Leaning over, the lawman struck her sharply across the mouth.

'I get you back in jail this time, I guarantee you'll talk!'

He released his grasp, allowed her to fall forward. Hovendon removed his hat, rubbed at his head. 'Beating the woman ain't getting us nowheres ... And I don't hold—'

'The hell with you,' Trask snapped, and swung his glittering eyes to Rapp. 'Get her on that horse, Joe.'

Pivoting, he pushed his way through the brush, returned to the trail. Della felt Rapp's hands about her waist as she was dragged upright. The foul smell of the man was sickening, and she tried to pull away.

'I'll help,' Hovendon volunteered, and stepped in close.

Weak from pain, Della caught at the saddle and hung there. Rapp, or Hovendon, or both—she neither knew nor cared—took her feet, boosted her onto the black. Rapp took the reins, and followed by the rancher, moved out of the arroyo.

Still dazed, she noted only vaguely the wounded man. He was holding one hand over a still bleeding injury in his shoulder while he spoke with Trask. The lawman was not listening but was, instead, staring up the trail. Dan would be up there somewhere—waiting; and now she would not be able to help him.

She wondered if he could see her, be foolhardy enough to come charging down upon them in an effort to free her. She hoped not. He'd have no chance against the four of them.

Rapp shuffled to the lawman's side, his eyes also on the upper slope. 'Well, what'll it be, Marshal? We going after him?'

'What's it like up there, Joe?' Hovendon asked.

'Be hell taking him, is he of a mind to fight. Could bed himself in the rocks, pick us off when we tried coming in. Reckon we'd get him, but you can figure on him getting a couple of us, too.' Rapp glanced meaningfully at the wounded deputy. 'He ain't no greenhorn with a rifle, that's for sure.'

'What he wants us to do, move in on him,' Trask said. 'Be a damn-fool thing to do even if we had plenty of men. Probably had this whole thing planned.'

'Planned?' Hovendon echoed.

The Marshal nodded impatiently. 'Sure—he went on ahead, hid the girl here. Figured we'd go on by, then she'd follow.

When we started closing in, she'd be behind us. They'd both open up, catch us in a cross fire.'

The rancher pursed his lips. 'Just what they had in mind, all right. Would've wiped us out.'

'And they'd have done it—for twenty thousand dollars ... Let's get mounted.'

Hovendon pivoted slowly to his horse, face knotted into a frown. 'You mean we're just pulling out? What about him—Reneger?'

Trask settled himself on his saddle. 'I ain't playing his game—he's going to play mine,' he said dryly. 'He finds out I got the woman again, he'll come down off that hill plenty fast.' Turning, he leered at Della. 'Way it is, sister—you're the honey that's going to catch me a big fly.'

$$\star \qquad \star \qquad \star$$

Why don't they come?
Dan Reneger shifted his position in the depths of the searing hot rocks and swore irritably. He'd been there an hour, and there was no sign of Trask and the posse. What the hell was holding them back? Could he have figured wrong? Was there a way out of the dead-end canyon after all—a trail that was permitting them to climb up, circle, and get above him?

He twisted about, and shading his eyes

161

from the sun's glare, carefully probed the ragged rim of the walls pocketing him. He saw no movement. There were no sounds of sliding gravel, displaced rocks. He shook his head angrily. No one was up there, and there'd been no trail—he would have spotted it.

He settled back, rifle laid before him, ready for instant use, and stared moodily at the opposite side of the tiny clearing where the trail made its entry. It was brushy on either side. The riders would likely leave their horses below, on the trail, work in on foot, using the scrub oak and thick-leafed mahogany as cover.

He could expect them to open up on him from both sides, probably two men to each corner. Or perhaps he'd be against only three guns; he had no idea how seriously he had wounded the deputy. One thing he could be certain of, however—if the man could pull a trigger, Emil Trask would make him fight.

It didn't really matter. He was in a hell of a spot regardless of how many men Trask threw against him. He might hold them off for a few minutes, but one of them was bound to get him, if not with a direct shot, then by a ricochet.

A ground squirrel darted from the lower end of the rock pile, paused, one black, beady eye fixed on the intruder of his domain. After a long minute, the small, striped animal, deciding there was no danger, ran into the open and raced for the far side of the clearing.

There was a sudden rushing noise as a hawk came out of nowhere, seemingly. Broad tail flared, wings set, talons extended, the killer swooped in. But the squirrel had reached sheltering brush, scampered to safety, and the hawk veered away.

The hunter and the hunted. It was a natural law, a system, and it affected everything that lived. He was no better off than that damned squirrel, Reneger thought; worse, in fact. He couldn't run, had no way to turn even if he wanted to. He had to stay there, backed against a wall, hunkered down in a pile of blistering rocks while his enemy closed in for the kill.

It was a hell of a system ... Man could get himself caught up in something he really was no part of and forfeit everything he'd ever hoped and dreamed of, including his life, just to round out the circle.

He stirred restlessly, angered by his thoughts. He didn't have to be where he was; he'd had a choice. Nobody made him go into Frisco Springs after Della Shofner and involve himself in something that was none of his concern.

Only, a man had to do what was right, and he knew the girl was innocent, that Emil Trask was a savage who'd delight in manhandling her. He couldn't turn his back on that ... Maybe he was a fool to throw everything away, but he couldn't see it otherwise.

*　　*　　*

Why didn't they come on?

He shifted again, sweat-soaked, eyes smarting from the burning glare, body aching. They should have reached the end of the trail long before then. He sat up, carelessly laid his hand upon the barrel of the rifle, jerked away with a curse when his skin came in contact with the heated metal. Brushing at his parched lips, he stared across the clearing. Everything lay silent, motionless in the driving sunlight.

Frustration swept him in a sudden gust. Seizing the rifle by the stock, he leaped to his feet. He'd force them to move in—he'd not stand this damned waiting any longer! He'd give them an easy target—anything was better than just sitting there.

No gunshots challenged his movement. He frowned. What the hell was Trask up to? Crawling from the rocks, he crossed open ground to the brush, ducked into its shadowy depths. They had him cold now if they were hiding somewhere close by. He'd never be able to make it back to the rocks once they opened up on him.

A jay, startled by his abrupt appearance, scolded from the branches of a pine, flitting back and forth, chattering noisily as its bright blue feathers flashed in the sunshine.

He waited until the bird quieted, then, on hands and knees, he crawled to the edge of the trail, peered from the undergrowth. The horses he expected to see waiting some distance below were not in evidence.

Disturbed now rather than angry, he worked his way through the brush alongside the trail. The clearing where the massive mound of boulders, and safety, lay was well behind him now, and if the fight started, he'd be forced to make his stand at that point ... It didn't matter. He was ready—anytime, anywhere. He was fed up with waiting.

Coming to the first bend in the path, he halted, sat back, muscles aching from the unnatural position he'd been in, sweat streaming down his face. He could see a full 100 yards down the slope—and there were still no horses ... And no sign of the posse.

All the anxiety, pent-up anger, and black frustration burst within him that next instant.

'Trask—damn you—come and get me!' he yelled, leaping to his feet.

The hills flung back his own words in a mocking, rebounding chorus. The sounds shocked him, made him aware of his act. He dropped into the depths of the brush, spun away in a quick change of position, and lay there, panting for breath.

Nothing ... Only the briefly silenced insects resuming their monotonous clacking, the far-off cooing of a dove.

He rose slowly, now sober and worried. Something had gone wrong. Ignoring further precaution, he strode to an outthrust of the slope where the trail swung wide and offered a view down the canyon to the flat lying far below.

Five riders—small dots moving east.

Realization came flashing to him. The trick had failed. Trask had discovered Della in the arroyo, had called off the chase, and was returning to Frisco Springs with her.

Dan Reneger's lips curled. The lawman was ignoring him deliberately—knowing well he would follow ... And he'd be waiting, this time on his own ground, on his own terms.

CHAPTER TWENTY-ONE

Sunset was not far off when Dan Reneger reached the fringe of Frisco Springs. He had ridden hard, alert for, but not expecting, an ambush, and he had encountered none. Emil Trask was confident he'd follow, and he was setting things up to suit himself.

Halting in the shadows at the end of the

street, Dan studied the strip of dust separating the twin rows of business buildings. Only a half dozen or so persons were abroad at the supper hour. No lamps had yet been lit, and the reflection of the red glow in the west laid a flaming sheen on the store windows.

He'd tried to figure what Trask would have in mind for him, what sort of trap he could expect. Would there be hastily sworn deputies stationed in the narrow passageways between the buildings along the street—possibly even on the roofs?

He doubted that. The lawman knew he would come seeking Della—and since Della undoubtedly would be within the jail, it was logical to assume that whatever trap had been set would be at that location. And Trask would want it to be all his show ...

Sam Lavendar, broom in hand, appeared on his front landing and began to sweep away the day's accumulation of litter. A small boy with a shaggy, panting dog crossed the street near the Frisco Springs Restaurant and disappeared into the lengthening shadows alongside ... He'd not do exactly as Trask expected, Reneger decided abruptly. The lawman would be looking for him to move in from the rear of the jail, take advantage of the dark, cluttered alley. He'd do the opposite.

And then?

Dan frowned. He hadn't taken time to think that far in advance, work up any plan. In the rush of anger following the discovery that Della was again in Trask's hands, he'd thought of one thing only—help her. But what came after that, assuming he was able to effect a rescue?

Take Della and run for it ... That appeared to be the only solution open. Only this time, they'd not head into the hills; they'd do a bit of circling, cover their trail, and line out for the nearest town. There, he'd put Della on the first stagecoach, regardless of its destination, place her beyond Trask's reach—and then he'd think about himself.

Mexico ... That was a good place for a man to lose himself and find protection from the law. He grinned bleakly at the phrase: *protection from the law*—it was supposed to be the other way around!

He glanced again to the sun. It was lost now, dropped below the horizon, leaving only a vast bank of blazing yellow shot with purple streamers. Turning the bay, he cut about, backtracked to the alley, and made his way behind the buildings until he was only a few doors from the jail.

Dismounting, he tied the gelding to a sagging hitch rack, drew his pistol, and started up the passageway separating two close-by structures for the street. A sudden hammer of hoofbeats brought him to a halt. He listened to the slackening drum, and then when it ceased somewhere along the street, he continued. A late customer trying to reach one of the stores before closing, he guessed.

Gaining the corner of the building, he stopped, swung his glance to the right and left. A horse stood in front of Lavendar's store ... That was the rider he'd heard coming in. He shifted his attention to the jail. No horses were at the rack, but a lamp burned inside. Reneger considered that. Had Trask taken Della elsewhere?

The possibility seemed remote. Trask, not particularly popular with the citizens of Frisco Springs and realizing he'd get little if any help from them, would play a lone hand. And the jail was his sphere, a private world where he'd concentrate all things pertaining to him. Della's horse had been taken to a stable by some sympathetic onlooker. That would explain its absence.

That wasn't good. They'd have no time to spare if he managed to free Della. Being forced to hunt up her black and saddle him would consume critical minutes ... He'd simply have to take the first horse they encountered, once started.

Reneger grinned at that prospect. He'd be labeled a horse thief, but he guessed when it was over, it really didn't matter. He would be in so deep by then that one more charge would count for little.

Checking the roofs and windows of the buildings facing the jail, and pistol in hand, he moved away from the corner. Stepping onto the sidewalk, he walked directly for the open doorway of Trask's office. Reaching the front wall of that building without incident, he once more halted.

Suspicion began to nag him. He'd expected opposition by that moment— deputies lying in wait, Trask himself positioned where he could watch, declare himself in at the proper instant. Instead— everything seemed deserted. Wheeling, Dan doubled back along the side of the jail to its rear. No one there—and no horses, either. Moving to a closed door, he put his ear against it and listened.

Silence ... The belief within him that Della had been taken to some other place of hiding presented itself again ... Trask had known he would head straight for the jail—was not making it so easy for him, after all ... At that moment, he heard a faint creaking.

He stiffened. Someone was inside. He was certain of that now, but whether it was Della or the lawman and his deputies there was no way of knowing. He moved on, completely circling the structure. If only he could be positive the girl was in there. He was reasonably sure now that she was, but there was an outside chance this was Trask's snare—that only he and his men would be inside, waiting—and if that proved true, he'd be putting his neck on the block for nothing ... Dead, he'd be of no help to Della.

There was only one way to find out, and time was slipping by fast. What he intended to do—walk in, blast a path of freedom for Della, and escape—should be done before there were many persons on the street.

Once again on the sidewalk, he looked toward the center of town. Two men were standing in front of the café, idly picking their teeth. Sam Lavendar and his nearly late customer were coming off the porch of the general store, probably aiming for the Nugget and a sociable drink.

Reneger took a long breath, turned the corner, swiftly crossed to the doorway of the jail. Hesitating, he listened. There was a dead hush. Bunching his muscles, he hurled himself through the doorway, dodged quickly to one side, his eyes sweeping the dimly lit room in a rushing search. The office was empty ... But he'd heard a sound—a chair or something scrape—

Movement in the shadows of the cell at the back of the room brought him up sharply. He whirled. In the weak light, he saw a figure move forward, press against the bars.

'Dan!'

It was Della. Relief shot through him. He

crossed to her in a single stride, peered at her anxiously. 'You all right?'

She nodded hurriedly. 'You've got to get out of here—it's a trap, Dan! They've been waiting—'

'Where?' he demanded, and whirled, hearing a faint sound.

'Right here,' Emil Trask drawled, his shape filling the doorway. In his hands he held a shotgun. 'Been watching you from across the street. Took you a hell of a long time to make up your mind.' The lawman paused, ducked his head at Reneger's pistol. 'Forget that ... One wrong move and you and your lady friend'll get both barrels.'

Dan lowered his weapon slowly. He'd been tricked neatly. He'd been a fool, he supposed, to think he could just walk in, shoot it out with whoever was around, and escape. But there'd been no other course to follow. Failure hitting him hard, he leaned against the cell, heard Della sigh in hopeless resignation.

'I'm sorry—dragging you into this,' she murmured. 'Told you before—don't be,' he said, and watched Trask come into the room, the twin muzzles of his shotgun never lowering. Immediately, Cal Hovendon and one of the deputies, both with cocked pistols, appeared. The rancher grinned, bobbed his head.

'Like you said, Marshal. She was the

honey that drew the fly.'

'Keep him covered,' Trask said, releasing the hammers of the shotgun and standing it in a corner. 'Shut that door, Sid.'

The deputy backed to the entrance, kicked the panel closed with his heel. Trask, moving in a slow, casual way, removed his jacket, draped it across a chair. The skin was pulled tight over the bones of his face, and his eyes glittered in the subdued lamplight.

'Now we'll get down to business, find out where that money's stashed,' he said.

Hovendon stared. 'You aiming to try making him talk?' he asked incredulously.

'Just what I figure to do.'

The rancher swore. 'Be a waste of time. Even I can see that.'

'He'll talk,' the lawman said confidently, 'when he sees me working a few Apache tricks on the girl ... Get his gun, Sid.'

The deputy started forward, hesitated as the door behind him opened. Sam Lavendar and the man Reneger had seen on the porch with him stepped into the room. The merchant's glance made a swift circle of the room, and then he shook his head.

'You can forget these folks, Marshal. We've found the money.'

CHAPTER TWENTY-TWO

Emil Trask did not move, simply stared at Lavendar, his small, red-rimmed eyes unblinking. Cal Hovendon was the first to break the charged hush.

'You found the money—where?' he asked, reaching for the satchel the merchant carried under his arm.

Lavendar surrendered the bag. 'My boy here come across it,' he said, motioning to the younger man with him. 'Was working around the old Sierra place—I aim to rent it out. Found the satchel near that old 'dobe wall.'

'Was all heaped over with leaves and such,' Lavendar's son said.

Hovendon was pawing hurriedly through the bag's contents. 'Looks like it's all here,' he said, looking at Trask. 'Reckon we was all wrong about Reneger and the lady.'

The Marshal shook his head slowly. 'Don't see where it changes anything.'

Dan Reneger stiffened. The load that had slipped from his shoulders suddenly was there again.

Lavendar's brows arched. 'Why? Proves they had nothing to do with it.'

'Proves nothing! They just hadn't got a chance to go pick it up.'

174

The merchant swore in disgust. 'Use some sense, Marshal. If they'd known where it was hid, they'd have swung by and picked it up when they lit out last night. Was right on the way—not fifty yards off the trail.'

Hovendon, all smiles, nodded. 'He's right, Emil. They sure wouldn't have took off leaving twenty thousand cash behind.'

'You're all a pack of damned fools!' Trask exploded suddenly. 'They're taking you in—laughing at you right now!'

'Seems you're the fool,' Lavendar said coolly. 'Tried to tell you they didn't have anything to do with that holdup, but like always, you were too bullheaded to see it anything but your way.'

Trask, flushing angrily, drew himself up to his full height. 'I know what I know ... And I'm the law here.'

'Even if you do get yourself locked up in your own jail once in a while,' the younger Lavendar said, grinning.

'... And nobody's telling me how to do my job.'

'And I'm the elected mayor of this town,' Sam Lavendar said in the same controlled voice. 'I'm ordering you to release these people—drop all charges if you ever had any—and let them go on their way.'

The lawman's head wagged stubbornly. 'Not a chance. You're forgetting he's an outlaw—wanted—'

'You forget it,' the merchant cut in coldly. 'We've caused him enough trouble. We'll not cause him more. Best thing you can do—'

'No, goddammit!' Trask shouted, eyes blazing wildly as he reached for his pistol. 'I'll never let—'

Reneger, weapon still in hand, fired from the hip. The small room rocked with the concussion. Smoke boiled up in a pungent cloud. Trask, standing at such close range, slammed back under the bullet's impact, fell against his desk, and slid to the floor.

'Dan—no!'

Della's agonized cry was only a sob. He knew instantly she was thinking of the consequences of his act, its bearing upon his future. It had appeared that his accidental brush with the law was going to be passed unnoticed, thanks to Sam Lavendar's consideration, but now he'd killed a man—a lawman. And for him, despite the fact that it was in self-defense, the result would be ruinous.

As well finish it, end it, he decided abruptly, watching the merchant rise after his brief examination of Trask. They'd never get the chance to turn him in; he'd never let them put him behind bars ... And Della was safe now ... He need worry no longer about her.

Taut, gun leveled, he faced the other men.

'I'm pulling out,' he said quietly. 'See that the lady gets put on a stage for her home.' He paused, added. 'Nobody tries to stop me—nobody gets hurt. That clear?'

Sid, hand resting on the butt of his revolver, stood rigid. Hovendon clutched the satchel to his side as if fearing to again lose it. Only Sam Lavendar moved.

Raising his hand carefully, he said: 'Put it away. You're among friends, Reneger.'

Dan eyed the merchant closely, uncertain whether to trust him or not.

'I mean it,' Lavendar said. 'Don't like killings, and it's a hell of a thing this had to end up the way it did. Was bound to happen to Trask someday, though.' He turned to the deputy. 'I'm naming you the new marshal, Sid. Get the keys, let the lady out of there.'

The lawman hastened to comply. Slowly, Dan slid his pistol into its holster. Lavendar waited until Della was free and had moved to Reneger's side.

'Trask told me he figured to get you somehow—even if he couldn't prove you were in on the holdup. He hated your guts.'

'And you? What you intend to do?'

'Can't say as I need to do anything. Nobody else around here either.' The merchant paused, touched each of the men in the room with a stern glance. 'Want that understood. Nobody knows anything—and if any of you forget—I got ways—'

Sid and young Lavendar nodded. Hovendon patted his satchel. 'Only thing I was interested in—getting this back.'

Reneger, practical, and perhaps more experienced in such situations, pointed to Trask. 'Appreciate all that, but what about him?'

'He'll get buried,' Lavendar said laconically. 'Word'll get out that he was killed doing his duty. Afraid that'll make quite a few people happy.'

Dan shrugged doubtfully. 'Maybe so, but he was a lawman. There'll be questions asked.'

'Your name won't be in the answers. I figure the town owes you that much.'

'Owes him plenty,' the younger Lavendar observed.

The merchant wheeled to his son. 'All right, then, let's be damn sure—all of you—nobody ever knows what happened in here tonight!'

Sid scratched at his jaw. 'But what'll we say—'

'The stage was held up, and there was a killing. Man by the name of Shofner done it. The Marshal—Trask—hunted him down. There was a gunfight. Now they're both buried out there in the graveyard. We don't need no more explanation than that. If there's somebody comes along who ain't satisfied—send them to me.'

Sam Lavendar mopped at his face, glanced at the men before him. 'Any questions?'

There was only silence.

'Then it's over and done with,' the merchant said with finality.

★   ★   ★

Della and Dan Reneger halted that next morning at the edge of town. The sun was just above the eastern horizon and already was beginning to make itself felt. They'd had a good rest at the hotel, eaten their first full meals, and Reneger had found time to shave, clean up a bit.

It had been his thought to ride out early, wishing to be well away from the settlement before the news of Emil Trask's death spread. There was no danger of retribution, as such, he knew, but questions would be asked, and if the answering were left to the autocratic Sam Lavendar and the new marshal, there'd be no leaking of the truth.

'Figured I'd swing back to camp, collect the mules and my gear, then head north,' Dan said. 'If you're willing to take time, come along, I'll ride on with you to the next town.'

Della studied his hard cornered face thoughtfully. His skin looked scrubbed and faintly blue where the beard had been scraped.

'Shame you can't stay there. It's a fine place. Your ranch would do well.'

He shrugged. 'No doubt, but Frisco Springs is too close. Somebody looking at me one day would remember, say something ... And then trouble would come.'

Della smiled. 'Perhaps ... You don't put much faith in others, do you?'

'Had my lessons,' he said, looking away.

'Isn't there anyone—anyone at all you think you could trust?'

He swung to her immediately. 'You,' he said in a hurried way, as if anxious to get it out. 'Della—come with me ... We can make a life together—I know we can! Maybe I haven't the right to ask, with trouble hanging over me like a black cloud ... And maybe it's wrong, with Luke dead only a few days, but I need—'

'None of that matters,' she broke in gently, laying her hand on his arm. 'What's past is past—and behind us.'

Dan Reneger grinned. 'Let's go find those mules. We'll need them if we're starting over again.'